Dedicated with love and appreciation
to 'fancier' Neil Neufeld,
my former pastor and long-time friend,
and to his dear wife, Gladys.
May God continue to bless you both.

Table of Contents

Chaper One

The Dilemma

"Where is he anyway?"

The plump, blue-gray bird tapped his foot impatiently and scowled at the sun high in the sky.

"He has never been late before," a soft voice beside him dared to comment.

"No—and there's a reason for it now," shot back the larger bird. "It's way, way past breakfast. He must know we're starving."

Blue Boy looked slyly at the large pigeon, wishing that he dared to say what he was thinking. Goliath, the plump blue-gray pigeon did not look like someone who was starving. His full body showed that he ate with regularity—and ate well. In fact, Blue Boy reminded himself, Goliath always saw to it that he got more than his share of the morning's feeding. Blue Boy decided to move away from the flock-boss a short distance so he would be sure to hold his tongue. Already Goliath was in a foul mood, and Blue Boy had no desire to feel the ravage of his sharp beak.

Blue Boy did not bother to unfold his wings for the

short distance up the side of the loft roof. He could walk that far. He bobbed his way toward the peak and positioned himself where he could watch the big yellow house where the man lived.

It was late! He should have been there with their breakfast. He had never been late before.

Blue Boy kept his eyes toward the house and settled himself comfortably on the peak of the roof—that is, as comfortably as one can, with a stomach insisting that it is way past breakfast.

The pigeons below him shifted around uneasily. The soft, contented cooing that usually marked the location of the flock had stopped. Instead, the voices now sounded irritated—worried. Where was the man with their breakfast?

A few of the younger birds took to the sky. They circled over the house and the entire property belonging to the birds and their man and then fluttered to a landing on the loft roof again.

"Did you see anything?" asked several of the older pigeons almost in unison.

"Nothing," they responded, just as the others who had flown over the house reported earlier. "Nothing. No one is stirring. There is no sign of the man anywhere."

A noisy chatter followed their news. It was Goliath who brought things back to order.

"Well, if he doesn't show up soon, I'm off. I'm not waiting around here for him any longer."

Mrs. Goliath made no comment. She was used to her husband's ranting and had long ago learned that things were much more peaceable if she pretended not to hear. She pecked absent-mindedly at some specks in the shingles on the roof.

But someone else dared to question Goliath. Molly Malone had never been slow to question anyone, and

she and Goliath had had many arguments over that fact. Still, she never seemed to learn—and now she challenged him again.

"Where will you go?" she asked with a flip of her head. "Goodness knows you know nothing about foraging."

Goliath gave her a cold, angry stare.

It would have stopped most of the pigeons from further comment, but not Molly.

"Suppose you'll join the elevator pigeons picking grain out of the dirt?"

Molly tossed her head again and looked scornfully at Goliath. The elevator pigeons were considered to be much below her status in the thinking of Molly Malone.

"No," snapped Goliath. "I happen to have friends at a few of the nearby lofts, though I'm sure you wouldn't have that advantage."

Molly ignored the barb.

"And I suppose your 'friends' have put aside a goodly portion of their breakfast just waiting for the privilege of your presence at their table."

She tilted her head and bobbed her neck slightly. Blue Boy could see that she was angry.

He switched his eyes back to Goliath. The big pigeon was glaring at Molly, his feathers lifting slightly to show his plumpness even more. He looked huge as he strutted toward the smaller, defiant female. Blue Boy held his breath. It looked like they would all witness another scrap between the two contentious birds, but just at the last moment, Mrs. Goliath stepped lightly between the two. She looked as serene and sweet as ever and with a calmness that made one think that she had heard nothing of the exchange between the two, she then addressed her angry husband with a soft voice—as though a thought had just suddenly come to her.

"Why don't we just take a little trip over to the park, dear? You know how the people over there love it when we visit."

For a minute it looked to Blue Boy like Goliath would push his wife aside and continue his argument with Molly—but then he hesitated. It was just long enough for Mrs. Goliath to divert Molly's attention.

"Have you been to the park recently, Mrs. Malone? It's so lovely there in early spring. They have given all of the benches a fresh coat of paint—and there are always so many of the older folk strolling the paths or feeding the birds."

Goliath's feathers began to relax again. He turned from Molly and headed back up to the peak of the roof. He wanted one more good look toward the house before he left for the park. After all, it was a fair ways to fly on an empty stomach.

Mrs. Goliath smiled sweetly at Molly Malone, complimented her on the shine to her neck feathers, and followed her husband up the roof.

She had more sense than to suggest the trip to the park again. She would wait for his decision on the matter. She knew his hunger would soon drive him to do something, and she also knew that when he took to the air in search of food, all of the other pigeons would be free to do likewise.

Goliath's eyes were still on the back door of the yellow house. Where was the man? Where was their breakfast? He couldn't wait much longer. But if he left, where would he go? He knew that Molly Malone had been right about one thing: the breakfast at the other lofts would have been eaten long ago. The humans who cared for the pigeons put out only enough food to nourish the birds—not fatten them. It was important— so the owners said—that the birds be strong, yet trim for flying. Flying seemed to mean so much to the humans.

Goliath stormed. He hated short rations. Not that he ever suffered, he saw to that—though this man had, in the past, locked him up for periods of time and cut back his rations to get him in 'flying' trim. Goliath could see no sense in it. With all that was needed right here at the loft, there was really no reason for him to do any flying anyway. Besides, he wasn't as young as he used to be, and flying was a bit more of a chore.

He did hope the food would come before he would be forced to journey all the way to the park. He did wish the man would tend to his business. It was all so aggravating. Was the man starving them all just to get them trimmer for flying? Goliath noticed that the man didn't expend any of his energy by propelling himself through the sky. Oh, no! He stayed right on the ground, conserving all of his strength.

Goliath looked steadily at the brown door in the splash of yellow that was the north side of the house. If the man didn't come soon, someone was going to have to do something. They couldn't just go on and on without eating.

He cocked his head and looked at the sky. The sun was almost directly overhead. It would soon be swinging to the west. Where was that man anyway?

He shot another glance toward Molly Malone. She was busy gossiping with one of the other women. Such a busybody, thought Goliath. Her tongue is never still.

He picked angrily at his leg band, a habit he had when he was upset. What an awful way to start the beautiful spring day. Why didn't someone do something?

Blue Boy watched all of the action from his perch near the peak of the loft. He was worried, too, that the man had not brought their breakfast. Now he was waiting for one of the older birds to suggest going out to look for something to eat. He was not above eating with the elevator pigeons if it meant getting something into his empty stomach. He had sampled some of their grain from the street dust in the past and it hadn't tasted so bad. Still, he didn't want to be the one to suggest it. Goliath might take exception and Blue Boy already knew better than to anger the big bird.

He'd wait. He'd wait if he had to, but he sure hoped it wouldn't be for too long.

Chapter Two

Neighbors

On the acreage next to Mr. Faraday, the pigeon owner, two pairs of eyes watched the goings on at the loft. Many, many times the two boys had followed the action of the pigeons. Many, many times they had longingly dreamed of having pigeons of their own.

They loved the birds and loved to watch their graceful circling as they went out for their daily exercise flights. They loved to listen to the chatter and cooing that took place on the roof of the loft. They loved to watch Mr. Faraday as he carried the birds their food and water.

But they did not love Mr. Faraday.

Mr. Faraday was a gruff, grouchy old man who seemed to have no patience at all with young boys, especially when they leaned over his fence, longingly studying his birds.

In fact, Mr. Faraday didn't seem to like people at all. He lived by himself and didn't welcome visitors. He never went out, except to get his mail from the metal box by the side of the road or to go to the local stores for food for himself and his pigeons.

He didn't like cats either—they chased birds. And he didn't like dogs—they barked and frightened his flock. His birds were registered—every one of them. Whenever he did put himself out to talk to any of the neighbors, he always made sure they knew that his birds were registered homing pigeons. Mr. Faraday dearly loved his pigeons.

Mark and Timmie loved the pigeons, too. But then, Mark and Timmie also loved cats—and dogs. They loved ponies and lambs and hamsters and rabbits. But Mark and Timmie had no pets—not one—not since Goldie their goldfish had died late last fall. And Mr. Faraday was the reason.

The house where Mark and Timmie lived was rented from Mr. Faraday. It wasn't a very fancy house, but it was the best that the boys' mother could manage on her salary since they had lost their father in a boating accident. And there was plenty of fresh air and room to run, and a big garden spot. There were even trees to climb, and Mark and Timmie could have been very happy on the acreage had it not been for gruff Mr. Faraday and his strict rules. "No pets," he said. And he stressed it over and over to the boys' mother. "Any pets and you are 'out', no second chances."

So Mark and Timmie could only crowd to the fence that separated the Faraday yard from the Thomas yard and studiously watch the pigeons.

But today as they watched the graceful birds, it was obvious something was wrong.

"What's wrong with 'em?" Timmie whispered.

"I don't know," responded his older brother, "but something sure is botherin' 'em."

"Do you see any cats?"

Mark studied the back yard carefully before answering.

"Nothin'," he said. "Not a movement anywhere."

There was silence for a moment. Both boys were thinking. Timmie voiced their thoughts.

"Do you see Mr. Faraday?"

"No," said Mark with a shake of his head.

"Have you seen the pigeons eat this morning?"

"No."

"Maybe they haven't been fed."

"He always feeds them first thing," and Mark studied the food containers to see if they had been filled that morning.

"I know," Timmie went on, "but maybe he ran out of food or somethin' and had to go for more."

"He never forgets to get food," Mark responded, showing a bit of impatience with his brother.

Just then some of the younger pigeons left their perch on top of the loft and circled the premises. They did not exercise in the usual way, circling just once and returning to the loft. A general chattering followed the fluttering of their wings.

"Something sure is wrong," said Mark. "They never act like that. They are upset about something."

"I still think they're hungry," cut in Timmie. "I think we should go see."

Mark gave him a dark, reprimanding look.

"And get ourselves in trouble—and Mom, too? You know Faraday said he'd skin us alive if he ever caught us on his property. He'd kick us out of the house—just like that—," Mark snapped his fingers to emphasize his point, "then where'd we be?"

Timmie said no more. He knew his older brother was right. Mr. Faraday had made the conditions of their stay in his rented house very clear. The boys were not to go near him or bother him in any way. And never—never—were they to bother the pigeons. Timmie turned from the fence.

"Let's play with our trucks in the garden," he said. "I don't want to watch the pigeons anymore."

Mark turned with him as they gathered their trucks and went to the end of the big garden patch that was still unplanted. With the warming of the chilly spring nights, the area would soon become garden. Then the boys would not be able to build roads and haul the dump truck loads of soil back and forth as they played with their Christmas construction set. They knew they should make each day count.

Mark became the foreman and Timmie the truck driver as the road began to take shape. The truck dumped load after load, and the Caterpillar pushed it around to level the roadbed.

Still, their minds were not totally on the road construction. They could still hear the fussing of the pigeons. Something was wrong next door. They both knew it, but they had no idea what to do about it.

Chapter Three

The Idea

The dump truck bumped to a stop, spilling some of its load of garden soil before reaching its intended curve in the new road.

"I know," shouted Timmie, "the mailman comes pretty soon!"

Mark straightened up from his crouching position over the Caterpillar and looked at his excited brother.

"The mailman," Timmie cried again. "Bet he won't be afraid to go on Mr. Faraday's property. He can check if somebody is home."

Timmie jumped to his feet and started for the road that ran past the two houses. Mark was right behind him. It might work. If Mr. Faraday was not at home, then maybe they could report the pigeons to . . . well to . . . to somebody. And then maybe they would come and feed them.

As the boys ran toward the road, the pigeons flew skyward, frightened by the sudden action next door.

"Walk," cautioned Mark reaching out a hand to slow Timmie down. "You're scaring 'em."

Timmie walked, but inside he felt agitated. He knew without even looking at the clock that it was almost time for the mailman to make his morning call.

And then they heard it, the low hum of the mail jeep. They ran again, in spite of the pigeons.

They were too late. When they reached the road, the dust of the mail jeep was swirling in the air, and the back of it was just disappearing around the bend toward the Engleson's.

"We missed it," said Timmie, flopping disappointedly into the grass beside the road.

Mark plopped down beside him. Idly he picked up small gravel stones and tossed them in the direction that the jeep had disappeared.

"What do we do now?" asked Mark. It was unusual for him to ask his younger brother for advice, but because of his concern about the pigeons, Mr. Faraday and the missed mailman, Timmie did not even think to notice.

"We should go check. That's what I think. The pigeons wouldn't act like that if there wasn't something wrong."

"But what could be wrong?"

"They're hungry—that's what."

"I know—I know," interjected Mark, "anybody can see that. But why? Why are they hungry? Mr. Faraday always feeds them first thing."

"Maybe he forgot."

"He doesn't forget."

Mark and Timmie walked slowly back down the lane and leaned over the fence to study the pigeons. The restlessness of the birds continued, and the frowns on the faces of the boys deepened. For several minutes they watched in silence, and then Timmie picked up the conversation just where they had left off.

"Maybe he's getting them ready for a race."

"He doesn't get them ready by starvin' 'em. Besides when he wants to limit their food, he shuts them up in their own little houses."

"Maybe he's sick," said Timmie, desperate to come up with an answer.

"That's it!" shouted Mark, jumping to his feet. The pigeons lifted off the roof of the loft with a terrible commotion.

"He's sick. That's it. It's got to be. He wouldn't let anything else stop him from carin' for his pigeons."

Timmie looked at his excited older brother. Maybe Mark was right. Maybe not. But what could they do about it if he was?

"We've got to do something," Timmie said softly. "He might be sick—bad. Or hurt or somethin'. Maybe he has a broken leg or a—."

But Mark didn't let him finish.

"The rule still applies," he cautioned. "We still can't go barging over there onto his property. Mom wouldn't like it, an' Mr. Faraday would get real mad."

"But if he's sick—or hurt—."

"Doesn't matter," said Mark stubbornly.

"We shoulda caught the mailman—," cut in Timmie. "If you woulda let me run—."

"You wouldn't a been there in time anyway," Mark put it, not willing to take the blame for the mailman getting away. "He had already put the mail in the box."

Timmie's face brightened.

"Let's go get his mail and take it to him. Then he will—."

"Don't be dumb," said Mark. "He wouldn't want us touchin' his mail either."

"Well, we gotta do somethin'."

"What?"

"I dunno. But we can't just let him lay there—if he's

sick or hurt.''

''Well, we can't get thrown out of our house either. Think how Mom would feel.''

''Well, Mom wouldn't want an old man to be left all alone if he was sick, either—even if it was taking chances,'' continued Timmie, and Mark knew that Timmie was right. Their mom would never leave an old man lying sick or hurt just to save her rented house, even if that house was very important to her.

''Come on,'' he said to Timmie, grabbing him by the sleeve. ''We'd better get over there and see what's wrong.''

It was frightening to walk up the path to Mr. Faraday's simple, yet neat, little yellow house. The boys had never been in his yard before.

As usual the pigeons were disturbed by the presence of strangers, and they took to the sky again, grumbling and complaining as their wings beat against the warm spring air to lift their bodies into flight.

When the boys reached the door, Timmie stepped slightly behind his older brother, his eyes dark with fright. Mark took a deep breath, stretched his neck to try to see in the curtained window, then rapped lightly on the door. Both boys were poised to run at a moment's notice if the need should arise.

There was no response to the knock, so Mark got up his courage and knocked again, louder this time. There was still no response.

''He's not here,'' Timmie whispered, relief showing in his voice.

Mark knocked again—loudly this time, and waited for a moment.

''See,'' said Timmie again. ''He's not here.''

''Maybe he just can't come to the door,'' ventured Mark.

Timmie's eyes filled with horror.

"You think he's *that* sick?" he questioned.

"Might be. If he hasn't fed his pigeons, he's pretty sick alright."

They stood motionless for a moment, each shuffling through his own thoughts.

"What do we do now?" asked Timmie.

"I dunno. Maybe we should feed the pigeons."

It was a scary thought.

"What if we feed them wrong—too much or not enough or somethin'."

"That might be better than them not gettin' fed at all."

"I dunno."

They stood quietly for a few more minutes.

"Maybe we should get help."

"Who?"

"A policeman or somethin'."

"He'd sure be mad if we got a policeman an' he's okay."

Silence.

"Let's look."

"How?"

"He's got a step ladder somewhere. I've seen him use it. We'll put it to the window."

Both boys bounded off the porch and went in search of Mr. Faraday's ladder. They found it hanging on the side of his grain shed. It took them both to carry the ladder and position it beneath a window, then as Timmie steadied it, Mark climbed up to peer in the window.

"Can you see anything?" whispered Timmie hoarsely.

"Naw, he's got the curtain pulled."

Mark climbed down and they tried another window. That curtain, too, was drawn. Round the house they went —window by window. They were about to give up when

Mark mounted the ladder to peek in the last window. There on the kitchen floor he could see the legs of a man protruding out from behind a section of cupboard.

"It's him!" he fairly shouted to his brother. "He's on the floor!"

Timmie forgot to hold the ladder as Mark came scrambling down, and in their excitement they nearly had an accident. Mark jumped clear and the ladder toppled over on its side.

"We gotta put this back before he sees us," said Timmie, grabbing the ladder and starting to drag it across the yard to the shed.

"You silly," said Mark, "He's not gonna see anything. Didn't ya hear me? He's layin' on the floor. He's hurt—or sick—or maybe even dead."

Timmie stopped dragging the ladder and looked at his older brother.

"We better git!" Timmie said, his eyes big with horror. "They might think we did it."

"Don't be dumb," said Mark. "He needs help—we gotta do somethin'."

Without further comment the boys heaved the ladder back up to its position on the side of the shed.

"What can we do?" asked Timmie.

"Let's try the door an' see—."

"I'm not goin' in there—not me," said Timmie.

"We've gotta help him."

Timmie nodded, but his throat still felt dry with fear. Together they moved to the door. Mark stepped forward and tried the knob. It would not turn. They ran around to the back and sent the pigeons scurrying again. That door, too, would not open.

"What do we do now?" Timmie puffed.

"We'll have to phone."

"We don't have a phone."

"No, but the Englesons do," answered Mark.

"It'll take too long—."

"That's all we can do. You ride your bike and get them to phone an ambulance or somethin'."

"Aren't you comin'?"

Mark shook his head.

"What you gonna do?" asked Timmie.

"I'm gonna give these poor birds some breakfast," responded Mark, and started toward the grain shed.

Chapter Four

Breakfast

The hungry pigeons were even more alarmed when the intruders from next door entered their yard. They had been used to seeing the boys busily playing in the yard next door or hanging over the fence watching their activities, but they had never seen them threaten their safety by actually coming into the yard of the man.

Their presence there now, troubled the birds. It was all wrong—all wrong. The man should have come out of the brown door and gone to the grain shed long ago. Their breakfast and cool drink of water should have been served to them before the sun climbed up into the sky.

No breakfast had come. No sign of the man had been seen. And now here were these intruders, noisily climbing all over the property that belonged to the man.

Again and again the pigeons took to the air, but their hunger—and their curiosity—quickly brought them back to the loft roof again to see what might transpire. Would the boys rouse the man? Would he now bring their breakfast?

Goliath took charge of the nervous flock.

"Settle down now. Settle down," he scolded them. "We don't want to frighten the boys away. Let's see if they can find the man."

The pigeons fluttered to a halt and rather noisily turned to watch the activity at the house. Surely the man would soon come out, issuing threats and unpleasant sounds. He always did if the boys got closer than he desired. But the door of the house did not open.

Then one of the boys left the house on the run, and in spite of the admonition from their leader, a number of the pigeons fluttered nervously, changing positions and murmuring to one another.

"Sh-h-h," said Goliath in an angry tone. "You've frightened off one of them—now be quiet before the other one leaves, too."

Molly Malone whispered her protest, "I wish they would both go. They shouldn't be here and you know it. The man will never—."

"Quiet," said Goliath as he looked glaringly at her.

Molly moved away, but she was still muttering under her breath.

Blue Boy held his tongue. He didn't share the feeling of Molly. He had always rather liked the boys next door. They had never threatened him; in fact, he wasn't aware of them threatening any of the birds. He watched as the boy who remained, the bigger one of the two, walked slowly toward the shed where the pigeons' grain was kept.

The boy tried the door, but it wouldn't open. Mr. Faraday always kept the shed locked.

Mark hesitated, then looked around helplessly. Now what would he do? He didn't wait for long. At least, he decided, he could give them a drink of water. He found the garden hose and dragged it toward their watering

dish.

"What's he doing?" grumbled Molly Malone.

"Looks like he's putting some water in our dish," responded Mrs. Goliath in a soft whisper.

"That's the man's job," spat out Molly, and for once, Goliath agreed with her.

"He shouldn't be doing that," said the big bird. "I'll bet he doesn't even know how to fill it properly."

"Just the same," said Abner, a trim bird with an adventurous spirit, "it sure would be nice to have a drink." He clicked his beak in anticipation.

Mrs. Goliath simply nodded her head.

"He might poison us," put in Molly, cocking her head and looking suspiciously at the boy.

"Why would he want to do that?" asked Mrs. Goliath.

"How should I know?" Molly flung back in anger. "Humans do some very strange things—without reason."

The flock watched as Mark rinsed the water dish with the water from the hose and carefully refilled it. Then he ran to turn off the hose and wound it back up on its reel. After he had finished, he backed away and sat down under the shade tree that grew beside the yellow house. This was the very spot where the man sat after he had fed and watered the birds. As soon as the man took this position, the flock, with Goliath leading, would leave the roof and dip to the ground to feed and water.

Not so this morning. Though many pairs of eyes looked thirstily at the water dish, no one stirred. The eyes shifted from the water dish to Mark, back to the water dish, again to Mark, but not one pair of wings rustled.

Blue Boy waited for Goliath to make the first move. Goliath just shuffled uncomfortably back and forth, angry mutterings escaping his lips.

At last Mrs. Goliath could stand it no longer.

"Shall we go, dear?" she asked quietly.

"Not going," said Goliath.

"Aren't you thirsty, dear?"

Goliath glared at her. Of course he was thirsty. He was so thirsty that his tongue stuck to the roof of his mouth.

"I think I'll have a little sip—," began Mrs. Goliath, but he stopped her.

"You can't trust him," he said. "He might have put something in the water."

Mrs. Goliath looked shocked. She started to open her beak but closed it again. Blue Boy could see her eyes turn back longingly to the water dish.

Was everyone just going to sit there and let the water go untouched? It was unthinkable.

"You see!" said Mrs. Malone. "It is just like I said. He might have poisoned it." She nodded her head toward Goliath as though she was glad finally to have something they agreed upon. Goliath turned his back to her. He did not want to share with Molly Malone—not even an opinion—especially when he feared that the opinion might point him out to be a sissy, afraid of his own watering dish and the small boy next door.

Blue Boy could stand it no longer. With a light spring into the air he stretched his wings and drifted down to the offered water. He was so thirsty. The water felt so good as it trickled down his throat. He dipped his beak in again and swallowed some more.

By the time he was taking his third swallow, some of the other pigeons had joined him. They, too, were thirstily drinking from the water dish.

Goliath was the last one to come. He pushed some of the smaller birds aside and dipped his beak deeply into the cool water. Blue Boy heard him sigh with satisfaction. He drank again—more deeply. No one was paying any attention to the small boy now. No one but Blue Boy.

He glanced over at the boy and saw a warm smile light his face. There was something pleasing about the smile. It made Blue Boy feel excited. The birds all knew that they were loved by the man—but Mr. Faraday was not one to smile.

Chapter Five

Commotion

The pigeons did not really have time to drink their fill when there was an awful commotion. A small farm truck belonging to Mr. Engleson came puffing into the yard and a man jumped out slamming his door shut almost before the truck rolled to a stop. Seeing Mark sitting quietly in the shade of the tree, he called to him in an old creaky voice, "Where did you see Mr. Faraday?"

As Mark stood to his feet, the pigeons were once again in the air. This time they did not even stop at the loft, but with a great flutter of wings left the yard to circle widely in the bright sunshiny skies.

Mark looked after them, concern in his eyes. Would they come back? He knew they missed Mr. Faraday. He knew they were still hungry. He knew they had been badly frightened. Would they come back?

Timmie, whose bike had been tossed hurriedly in the back of the old pickup, was running toward the ladder on the shed.

"We used this," he called to the elderly neighbor. "Mark climbed up on it and looked in the kitchen window. He saw Mr. Faraday's legs. He was on the floor.''

"We're gonna have to git to him," said Mr. Engleson.

"We can't," Mark responded, a bit upset by everything. "The doors are locked." He turned to Timmie. "I told ya to phone for help," he said sharply.

"We did," Timmie quickly replied. "They said they will come right away."

"Then why does he want the ladder?" asked Mark, as Mr. Engleson pulled the ladder into position under the window. He crawled slowly and creakingly up the steps and peered in the window.

"I dunno. Guess he just wants to see for himself."

"There he is," said Mr. Engleson. "That's him alright. Layin' right there on the floor by the cupboard. Yep. That's Faraday alright."

Mark and Timmie exchanged glances. Of course he was there, just like they had said. They weren't ones for making up stories—especially stories about someone being in need of help.

"I sure hope they hurry," whispered Mark. His eyes again went to the skies. He was even more worried now—about both Mr. Faraday and the birds.

Timmie gulped. There were tears in his eyes. He turned to his older brother and reached out as he took his hand, pressing a little closer to him for assurance.

"At least they're not so hungry now," he said, letting his eyes follow Mark's to where the birds had disappeared.

"I didn't get to feed them," whispered Mark. "The shed is locked."

"But they were eating when we came back—."

Mark shook his head. "Just drinkin'. That's all. Just drinkin'. They were so thirsty, but they didn't get enough to drink either."

Mr. Engleson still stood on the ladder, his face pressed

against the window pane. Mark and Timmie wished he would crawl back down. They wished the ambulance would arrive to help the man inside the house. And they wished the birds would return—even if they didn't land. It would be so good to see them circling in the sky again.

"He moved!" shouted Mr. Engleson suddenly, making both boys jump with his abruptness. "He moved. I'm sure that I saw his leg move—just a bit—but he moved."

Both boys wished they could see in the kitchen window, but Mr. Engleson didn't look like he was about to share his ladder. He pressed his face back to the glass.

Just then a siren was heard in the distance.

"They're coming," said Mark.

Timmie tugged at his hand.

"We better get outta here," he prompted. "If they bring Mr. Faraday out an' he sees us in his yard, he'll be mad."

Mark nodded. They couldn't afford to have Mr. Faraday angry with them. He might even make them move away from the house that they were renting.

Before the siren propelled the ambulance down the long lane and alongside the Faraday house, both boys had quickly slipped over the fence and into their own yard again.

They tried to watch what went on, but it was difficult to see. Most of the action took place inside the house. Even the outside activity was screened by the house itself and the tall trees that surrounded it. It wasn't long until the ambulance was screeching its way down the lane again and the boys knew that Mr. Faraday was on his way to the hospital. Now what would happen to him? And what would happen to his pigeons while he was gone?

With a sick feeling in the pit of their stomachs they

turned back to their rented house. It wouldn't be long until their mother would be home. They could hardly wait. Their mom would feel pretty badly about Mr. Faraday, too, even if he was a cross old man.

Before they got to the door, they heard the sputtering of the old farm truck. Mr. Engleson was coming down their drive, sending up billows of dust from the wheels of the rickety vehicle. Before they could even ask their question, the old man hopped from the truck once again slamming the door. Mark was surprised it still held fast to the hinges.

"Fergot yer bike," he called out, and Timmie remembered he had left his bike in the back of the old truck. He sure hoped Mr. Faraday hadn't spotted it there.

Mr. Engleson lifted out the bike, and Mark went to assist him.

"How is he?" Mark asked shakily.

"Well, I tell you one thing," said the elderly man, "Mighty good thing for him that you fellas had yer wits about you. He could have laid there like that fer days."

"What was wrong?"

"He had him a stroke, I guess. Couldn't move none. Right there on the kitchen floor. Couldn't even reach the phone."

"Is he alright?"

"He'll be okay—I think. But he'll be in the hospital some, that's for sure."

Both boys stood holding their breath. If Mr. Faraday was going to be in the hospital for several days, what would happen to his pigeons—his registered pigeons? Would they starve? Would they fly off? Would they ever return?

It was Mark who spoke. "What about his pigeons?" he asked quietly.

Mr. Engleson glanced toward the loft. "Never thought of his birds," he said.

"They'll need to be fed," ventured Timmie. "They'll starve if no one feeds them."

"Or else fly away," added Mark. "That would make Mr. Faraday really sad. He loves his pigeons."

"Reckon he does," said Mr. Engleson shaking his head. "Bout all he ever talks about." He thought for a moment, then continued. "Never had me much love for pigeons. Know nothin' about 'em. Nothin' at all. You suppose you could feed 'em?"

"We can't," said Mark, "the feed shed is locked."

Mr. Engleson looked over at the small shed.

"I'll call the hospital tomorrow and see iffen he'll give me the key," he said and seemed to think that the matter was closed.

He moved toward the door of his little truck, but Mark stopped him.

"The pigeons are real hungry," he said anxiously. "They haven't been fed today and it's getting awfully late."

Mr. Engleson stood and looked down at his scuffed

shoes. He kicked a bit at a clump of dirt, and the boys could see that he was thinking.

"Alright," he said at last. "Guess we'll hafta drive in to the hospital and ask Faraday what he wants you to do. Come along."

The boys were all ready to climb into the truck when Mark thought of their mother.

"We can't go," he said. "Mom will be home soon, and she'll worry about us."

"Well, I can't understand no pigeon-talk," said Mr. Engleson. "If you want to be feedin' those birds, then you're gonna need to talk to Faraday yourself."

Both boys were concerned. What should they do? Someone needed to care for the birds. Someone needed to be home to explain to Mom. It was Timmie who broke the silence.

"You go Mark," he said. "I'll wait for Mom."

"But Mom says I'm not supposed to go off and leave you all alone," argued Mark.

They stood looking at one another. They both knew that it was important to obey their mother.

"Guess you'd better go, Tim," said Mark, "an' I'll stay."

Timmie shrugged, then walked slowly to the shivering truck. Mr. Engleson had not turned off the motor and it sputtered as it coughed and tried to keep running.

Mr. Engleson crawled in his side and put the truck in reverse. It quivered its way out of the driveway and headed for town.

Mark stood alone watching them go. As soon as the cloud of dust disappeared from his sight, his eyes traveled back to the sky. There wasn't a sign of the birds anywhere. He hoped with all his heart that it wouldn't be too late when they finally got to the feed in the feed shed.

Chapter Six

Instructions

Timmie was nervous all the way into town. He should have been nervous about the old truck and its driver, but he never even thought about that. All his thoughts were of Mr. Faraday. Would the man be angry with them for invading his privacy? Would he tell them to go on home and mind their own business? Would he say they all had to move out of the rented house because the boys had broken his rule and come onto his property?

Timmie hoped not—but he wasn't sure.

Then Timmie thought of the pigeons, and he worried some more. Had they left for good? Would they come back now that Mr. Faraday was not there to care for them? Would they even eat the food if the boys did get the key to the feed shed? Pigeons are smart. They can sense when strangers are around. They might fly away and not come back, even if Mr. Faraday did say that the boys could feed the birds.

The hospital was a big building. It was made of brick and sprawled over the early spring grass for blocks and blocks—or so it looked to young Timmie.

Timmie had never been in a hospital—except for being born in one—and he couldn't remember one thing about that. A boy from his first grade class at school had been taken to the hospital. He was there for a long time, and when he came back he had lots of strange things to tell. Most of the things didn't sound like much fun to Timmie. He wanted no part of a hospital. But he solemnly followed Mr. Engleson anyway, across the parking lot and into the big building.

People were moving about in the corridors. There was a nurse at the front desk looking carefully at the strange pair who walked toward her and asked if she could help them. Mr. Engleson tried to explain to the nurse about Mr. Faraday and the pigeons, but she didn't seem to understand what he was trying to say.

Finally Mr. Engleson gave up and pulled Timmie toward the door. Timmie wanted to protest. They were leaving and hadn't even seen Mr. Faraday.

But Mr. Engleson was smarter than Timmie had thought. As soon as the nurse was busy with someone else, Mr. Engleson jerked Timmie around and hurried to an elevator.

It was many elevator rides and many nurses' desks later that they finally found themselves on the fifth floor where they understood the stroke patients were cared for. A stiff nurse in a crisp uniform stopped them as soon as they stepped off the elevator.

"May I help you?" she said, but her tone did not indicate that she was anxious to help them.

"We are looking for Mr. Faraday," said Mr. Engleson.

"Mr. Faraday has just been admitted," said the nurse.

"We know that," Mr. Engleson replied rather proudly. "We are the ones who called the ambulance."

"I see," said the nurse slowly, but Timmie wondered if she really did.

41

"I'm afraid that Mr. Faraday isn't allowed visitors yet."

"We need to see 'im," Mr. Engleson said again.

"Children aren't allowed in the rooms," replied the nurse curtly.

Mr. Engleson jerked impatiently at Timmie's shirt. "This one's got to see 'im," said Mr. Engleson. "He needs to know how to feed his pigeons."

"I beg your pardon," said the nurse.

"His pigeons," Mr. Engleson said impatiently. "Timmie here, an' his brother, are gonna feed the pigeons. They're registered, an' Mr. Faraday sure would be upset if anythin' happened to 'em."

"I'm sorry, but Mr. Faraday won't be allowed visitors for—."

"We gotta see 'im. We came all the way into town to—."

"They'll die," said Timmie in almost a whisper. "They'll die or—or—fly away."

"I'm sorry—," the nurse started again, but now her eyes were on Timmie's face.

Big tears had gathered and threatened to spill down his cheeks. "I'm sorry," said the nurse again, and she reached in her pocket and pulled out a tissue just like Timmie's mother would have done. But before she could use it to wipe away Timmie's tears, he stepped back, brushing his hand quickly over his eyes. He was not a cry baby. He straightened his shoulders.

"I'm sorry," said the nurse again, and she tucked the tissue back in her pocket.

Mr. Engleson took a step toward the nurse. He was not to be intimidated by a lady in white, no matter how crisp her uniform—or her manner.

"Being sorry ain't helpin' matters none," he said firmly. "This here boy an' me, we come to see Faraday.

Now his pigeons need carin' for and he ain't in no shape to do it. Timmie here—.''

But Mr. Engleson's speech was stopped by a doctor who had come up behind them.

"Did you say pigeons?'' he asked.

Mr. Engleson wheeled around to face the new voice.

"Pigeons!'' he said, spitting out the word. "I said pigeons. Belongin' to Mr. Faraday. They need carin' for an' Mr. Faraday won't be—.''

"I know all about Mr. Faraday,'' cut in the doctor. "I just admitted him—and he was mumbling and fussing about his pigeons the whole time.''

"Course he was,'' fumed Mr. Engleson. "They ain't been cared for—that's why.''

"You'll care for them?'' asked the doctor hopefully.

"Me? No sirree. Not me. I don't cotton none to pigeons,'' said Mr. Engleson backing up a pace.

The doctor's face fell.

"He'll never get well while he's worrying over those birds,'' said the doctor. "I'll have to give him a strong sedative to put him to sleep just so he will stop his fussing. It appears he has not really been well for several weeks—just barely managing to keep going. He's already worried because his pigeons haven't been separated into their pens as early as they should have been, and now this—. I wish—,'' but the doctor got no further.

"I won't care for 'em,'' Mr. Engleson insisted, and pushed Timmie forward, "but this here boy and his brother are all anxious to be doin' it.''

The doctor looked down at the small boy before him. "Is that right, son?'' he asked.

"Yes Sir,'' said Timmie, nodding his head.

"Do you know about pigeons?''

Timmie couldn't truthfully say he knew about the

care of the birds, so he answered in another way. "Mark and I love pigeons," he said. "We always wish that we could have some."

The doctor laid his hand on Timmie's shoulder. "Come with me, son," he said as the nurse watched with a disapproving look in her eyes. The doctor led Timmie right into the strange-smelling room where Mr. Faraday lay upon the sterile-white bed. Mr. Engleson cast a triumphant look in the direction of the nurse, and followed them into the room.

Somehow, to Timmie, the neighbor man looked smaller than he had remembered him. There was not a scowl on his face either—just a very worried look. His eyes brightened when he saw the small boy.

"Mr. Faraday is having a bit of trouble talking right now," explained the doctor. He pulled a pad and a pencil from his pocket and took Mr. Faraday's hand.

"Timmie and his brother are willing to take care of your pigeons until you are feeling well again," explained the doctor. "He has come all the way into town to get instructions from you so they can care for them just as you would if you were able."

Timmie didn't know if he just imagined it, or if he actually saw tears in Mr. Faraday's eyes.

It took Mr. Faraday a long time to write down carefully the instructions about the basic care of the flock. When Mr. Engleson and Timmie left the hospital, Timmie carried, along with the carefully penciled notes, the key to Mr. Faraday's house and the directions of where to find the key to the feed shed.

It seemed to take the old farm truck a long time to cover the miles back home, and Timmie clasped Mr. Faraday's house key until his knuckles were white. He could hardly wait to get back so he and Mark could take care of the hungry 'homers.'

Chapter Seven

Caring

On and on the frightened pigeons flew, led by Goliath. He did not know where he was taking them. He did not know where they would find food for their hungry stomachs. He only knew something had gone terribly wrong with their world. The man was no longer there to care for them, and in his place was commotion and confusion. Both factors frightened the birds.

Never, as long as Goliath could remember, had there been one of the noisy, smoking monsters in the driveway that led to the man's house, except for Mr. Faraday's own faithful old Chevy, and he always ran that as quietly and slowly as possible. The pigeons had often spied these other creatures, but they had always stayed on the dusty road where the mail Jeep traveled. Well, today—today there had been two of them—right in the yard.

First the rattling old truck had come, scattering the thirsty birds in a wild-circling of beating wings. It had taken Goliath many minutes to get the flock back into some kind of order, and then as they circled back toward the loft, another screaming creature intruded upon the acreage, spilling dust in a cloud like Goliath had never seen before. Right up to the house it raced, and in a state of even greater fright, the pigeons took off once more.

What was happening to their world? Somehow Goliath sensed it all had something to do with the missing man.

Many of the older birds were becoming tired. Goliath himself felt that he couldn't travel much farther, yet he did not dare to stop. Where would they land? They were miles away from their familiar loft and still feeling they were in danger. Goliath fought to still the racing of his heart. He was winded from the flight, and traveling now, strictly on fear.

When the flock had first lifted off the ground near the water dish and taken to the air, Blue Boy felt an excitement like he had never felt before. He loved to fly. He loved to feel the strength in his wings. He loved to feel the coolness of the wind as it rushed against his breast feathers, allowing his body to slip smoothly through the air. He loved the view of the earth from way up in the sky where everything looked neat and clean and placed in orderly fashion. Blue Boy loved the exhilaration of flying.

After the birds had been flying for some time, clearly not circling back toward the loft—and yet appearing to go nowhere—Blue Boy, like all the other pigeons, began to get concerned.

The loft was back the way they had come, and their food was back that way. Oh, it was true the man had not fed them their breakfast, but Blue Boy was sure it would be there when the sun came up the next morning. Surely, the missing of their meal was just one day's oversight.

But even without the prospects of a meal, Blue Boy

wanted to go home. There was something deep within that told him that home was where he should be—where they all should be. Still, Goliath made no move to circle and return to the loft.

Blue Boy put on a burst of speed. He wanted to be nearer to the leader of the flock and see if he could determine just what plans their leader had.

Goliath was slowing down. It was noticeable to all the birds. It was not hard for Blue Boy quickly to close the distance between himself and the big bird.

Mrs. Goliath still flew steadily beside her mate. She wasn't sure of Goliath's plans either, but she would not question him. As they flew she studied the landmarks beneath her. She had never flown out this far before in a flying exercise. She was seeing new things beneath her. They passed over streams and ponds, they traveled over farm lands and city buildings. She noticed parks and pavement and playgrounds—and still Goliath kept flying. Even Mrs. Goliath was beginning to weary from the heavy exertion.

It was Molly Malone who complained first—and loudest.

"Where *are* you taking us?" she screamed above the rush of wind against their wings. When Goliath did not answer, she cried again, "This is nonsense! Do you expect to just fly until we drop, one by one, from exhaustion?"

Goliath just gave her an angry look as though he hoped she would be the first one to go. Secretly, he feared *he* might.

"We haven't eaten, you know," whined Molly. "I realize that you have plenty of 'reserve' there, but some of us are not—."

Molly did not get to finish her sentence. With anger making him bold, Goliath swooped and headed straight down for the land below. The rest of the flock swished down and followed him earthward.

They landed in a grain field. It had not yet been planted with a new crop, as it was still too early in the spring. There was not much that remained from the year before, only a few kernels of grain scattered among the stubble. The younger birds set about scavenging the ground as soon as they ceased the flutter of their wings.

Goliath gave Molly Malone an angry stare as she landed a few feet away from him, and promptly strutted off—anywhere to be away from her.

Molly was still panting from the long flight so she folded her wings carefully and positioned herself on the ground, shutting her eyes in an effort to catch her breath again.

Mrs. Goliath settled herself sedately, then followed her husband toward the edge of the flock. She made no comment, nor did she start to feed, until he, with his back to the others, began to brush aside dry straw in an effort to find some kernels of grain. Then Mrs. Goliath accepted his lead and delicately began to peck away at the straw as well.

Blue Boy lost no time. He was famished. As soon as the wings folded upon his back, he was searching for food among the stubble. He wasn't too sure just what he should be searching for. He was a young pigeon, and had never foraged before. He was used to a full dish of grain being set before the flock.

As he picked and pecked his way across the stubble, he found very little to his liking. It seemed what the farmer had missed in harvesting, the winter rodents had eaten.

By the time the flock felt rested from their flight, the sun had moved far to the west in the distant sky. In spite of the length of time they had spent looking for food,

none of the flock had a full stomach. They picked and poked and fumbled through the straw, but there was little to be had for nourishment. Mrs. Malone had had enough.

"This is even worse than eating with the elevator pigeons," she complained. "Why did you insist on bringing us way out here—for this? We would have done much better at the park near town—like your wife suggested—but oh, no. You had to have your own way."

Goliath just ignored her.

"Well, I'm going home. Back to the loft where I belong," stated Molly Malone. "If you want to be the leader—then you'd better get up there in the sky—and lead—because I'm going whether you lead or not."

She tilted her head, and her bright little black eyes sparkled.

"And—," she added, "I wouldn't be surprised that there will be those who join me."

It was a challenge to Goliath. He looked surly. Mrs. Malone was daring to take the leadership of the flock right out of his hands. Goliath knew it—and so did the rest of the flock. Would he chastise her? Ignore her completely? He was in a very difficult position and well knew it.

It was Mrs. Goliath who quietly came to his rescue.

"Oh, look Mrs. Malone," she cried. "Look at the delicious grain right here under these leaves."

Mrs. Malone was not only bossy; she was greedy. She hurried across to the place where Mrs. Goliath had pointed. It gave Goliath just enough time to call, "All birds aloft," and to life himself from the ground. He was in command once more, and Mrs. Molly Malone, along with all the other birds, moved to obey the command.

It took Mrs. Goliath just a few minutes of strenuous

flying to take her rightful place beside her husband at the front of the flock.

The birds did not even circle. Goliath headed straight for home. Straight for the loft. It was getting dark, and they well knew that the safety of the loft was what they longed for—even if no food was there to fill their still empty stomachs.

It was a long trip home. The landmarks below began to be hidden from their view. No longer could they see the fields, the playgrounds, the ponds. Everything below was clothed in darkness except the strange lights that flickered here and there.

It was all new to the birds. They were not used to flying at night. All their practice flights and exercise flights were done in the daylight. Even those older members of the flock, who had experienced the thrill of a long race, had not navigated by moonlight.

Still, Goliath moved them toward the loft. He knew just where to head in the darkness. He was tired, but he would not give up. Steadily, and without any wavering, he directed the flock toward home.

Blue Boy learned a new respect for his leader that night. It was a good lesson in perseverance for all the young birds and all the older birds were tired. Everyone was still hungry—yet none questioned their leader. Not even Molly Malone. No one wished to stop and rest. They had one thought, and one thought alone: to get back to the safety and security of their familiar loft.

Chapter Eight

Food

When Mr. Engleson dropped Timmie off by the road, he ran all the way down the dusty lane, clutching the sheet of instructions and Mr. Faraday's house key firmly in his hand.

His mother was home. She had already changed from her office clothes into her gardening duds and was busy bending over her garden patch preparing the soil for planting. Mark, too, was busy with a shovel.

"I've got it!" shouted Timmie before he reached the house and as he dangled the key for them both to see.

Mark came bounding toward him.

"How did you get that?" he asked.

Timmie was puffing from his run, so he just shook his head.

Their mother hugged him for a moment, with concern for what the boys had experienced showing in her eyes.

"I've got some milk and cookies," she told him. "Why don't we sit on the porch?"

They laid down their gardening tools and walked to the porch, Timmie still waving the key back and forth in front of their eyes.

Mark could not contain his curiousity.

"Where did you get it?" he insisted. "Where did you get the key?"

But their mother interrupted, "How is Mr. Faraday?"

"He had a stroke—an' he can't talk good—but the doctor says that he will get better," Timmie informed them.

"But where did you get the key? Boy, I bet Mr. Faraday would be mad if—."

"He gave it to me," cut in Timmie, "an' he gave me this, too," he hastened, spreading sheets of paper out on the floor of the porch.

"What is it?" asked Mark.

"The 'structions. The 'structions on how to take care of the pigeons."

"Why didn't he just tell you?" asked Mark.

"I told you—he can't talk good," repeated Timmie.

"Not at all?"

"He mumbles. He's awful hard to understand."

Mark looked at the sheets of paper.

"He's not so good at writing either," he commented.

"We'll figure it out," Timmie assured him, as the two boys bent over the pieces of paper.

"You still haven't told us much about Mr. Faraday," said Mrs. Thomas.

"Yeah," said Mark, his head jerking up. "Was he mad?"

"Boys!" said their mother in exasperation.

"He wasn't mad. He was just worried," Timmie was quick to answer. "He was so worried about his birds that the doctor was gonna have to give him lots of medicine so he would sleep. The doctor was glad to see me there—and so was Mr. Faraday—I think. But the nurse sure wasn't."

"What did she do?" asked Mark, anxious to hear all about Timmie's experience.

"She was gonna make Mr. Engleson and me go away without even seeing Mr. Faraday—but Mr. Engleson wouldn't go."

"Oh, my," said Mrs. Thomas, "the poor nurse."

The boys did not even notice the comment.

"Then what?" asked Mark.

"Then the doctor came along—an' he was glad to see us an' he took me right in to see Mr. Faraday. He has a funny bed and lots of tubes an'—."

"What did he say?"

Timmie stopped and looked at his older brother disgustedly.

"I told ya," he said, "he can't talk. He just writes."

"Well, what did he write then?"

"The 'structions. The 'structions 'bout how to care for the pigeons."

"An' he's gonna let us?"

"He gave us the key to his house didn't he?—an' he told me—on this paper—where to find the key to the feed shed, too."

Mark jumped up from where he was sitting.

"Then we'd better git," he cried. "They are awfully hungry and will be back soon lookin' for food."

"Boys!" said Mrs. Thomas, reaching out her hand to steady a glass of milk nearly tipped over in the scurry.

Mark halted.

"Sorry, Mom," he apologized. "May we?"

"Of course. Go feed the birds. But don't forget you still have some chores here, too."

"We won't," they called in unison.

Mrs. Thomas watched them go. She understood their excitement, since they loved the birds. They needed a pet, and she wished with all her heart that it was possible for them to have a dog or cat. But rules are rules, and Mr. Faraday had stated specifically that no pets were allowed on the premises. And her family needed the house. She would never be able to afford another place on her limited salary.

Mrs. Thomas sighed deeply and lifted herself slowly from the porch. There was still some garden to be cultivated before she would be able to plant the seed.

Mark and Timmie ran quickly to Mr. Faraday's house and used the key to enter his kitchen through the back door. There, right where Mr. Faraday had said it would be, hung the key to the feed shed. Mark spread the pieces of paper out on the kitchen table, and the two boys carefully began to work through the instructions that Mr. Faraday had painstakingly written.

"We need to hurry before the pigeons get back," said Mark. "They could come anytime, and if they see us, they might still be scared."

Taking their instructions with them, they went to the feed shed and identified the various feeds.

When they had the feed mixed 'just right,' they placed it in the pigeon food containers, locked the shed door against any intruders, and carefully hung the key back on the hook by the kitchen cupboards. Then they put fresh water in the water dish and headed home to watch for the return of the pigeons.

All the rest of the day while they worked with their mother in the small garden, the boys eyed the sky. There was no sign of the birds returning.

Finally, the boys were called inside for bed. Mrs. Thomas saw their troubled looks.

"They'll come," she said brightly,. "Homers always return home to their own loft."

"But it's almost dark," said Timmie sadly. "They won't even be able to see where to fly."

"They'll come," she said again. "I don't know how they do it, but the darkness won't keep them away."

"I hope not," whispered Timmie and he went to the kitchen window to look out at the empty loft one last time. "I wonder if they are still scared and lonely."

Mark stirred beside him and looked out at the loft, too. It seemed strange for the windows of the neighboring house to be dark. Mr. Faraday had always been at home in the evenings—ever since the Thomases had moved into the rented house.

"I wonder—I wonder if Mr. Faraday is scared and lonely, too," said Mark.

Timmie turned to his brother, his eyes big with wonder.

"Do you really think he might be?" he questioned. "He's a man—he wouldn't get scared."

"Oh, my," said Mrs. Thomas. "Being grown-up doesn't mean you don't get scared anymore. I think it's very likely Mr. Faraday is scared—and lonely. He loves his pigeons. He must be worried about them—even when he knows you are caring for them."

"Why was Mr. Faraday always so mean, Mom?" asked Timmie. "If he was lonely, then why wasn't he nice to people so they would want to be nice to him?"

"I can't answer that, Timmie. But I do know that sometimes things happen in life that make people shut out other people—things like big hurts, disappointments, unhappiness. If we hold on to bitterness or pain, we can shut out happiness, too. We become afraid to be friends with anyone for fear we might be hurt again."

"Do you think Mr. Faraday was hurt?"

"I don't know, Mark. But I do believe Mr. Faraday was *hurting*. He was a very unhappy man."

There was silence for several minutes, and then Mark spoke thoughtfully.

"I'm glad we helped him—aren't you, Timmie?"

"Yeah," said Timmie. "I'm glad, too. Only—."

"Only what?" prompted Mrs. Thomas.

"Only I wish there was more we could do."

"You are doing more. You are caring for his pigeons and that is very important to Mr. Faraday."

"And we can visit him in the hospital, too," went on Mark. "We can tell him how his pigeons are doing, and that will make him happy—if they come home again."

Mark frowned as he thought of the sorrow Mr. Faraday would feel if his pigeons did not return.

Timmie still did not cheer up. He thought of the old man as he had last seen him, lying small and white upon his hospital bed, tubes and straps fastened to his body. He no longer looked frightening. He no longer looked mean. He only looked scared. Scared and worried.

Surely there was something more they could do for him.

Then Timmie's small face lit up.

"I know," he said. "Let's pray for him. Let's pray that he will get better quick—and that he won't worry about his pigeons—and that the pigeons will all come home safely, too."

Mrs. Thomas smiled, and Mark slapped his younger brother on the back.

"Good idea," he said. "Let's."

So they did.

Chapter Nine

Adjustments

It was very late when the pigeons got home to the loft, and they were all tired from the long flight. Even the younger birds were ready to admit that they had had enough exercise for one day. Some of the older birds were obviously exhausted. Goliath himself, though big and strong, had allowed himself to get out of shape. Blue Boy felt the older bird had made it home on sheer determination.

There was no chattering or arguing as they filed one by one into the loft pen. They were too tired for that. Even Molly's tongue was still. Her wings drooped and her eyes revealed pain from the sustained effort of the flight.

The moon was in the sky, though it only peeped out from behind the clouds now and then. The birds had little light to guide them as they took their places, silently, on the perches. Blue Boy had the feeling the night was not going to be long enough, and he supposed the other birds shared his thought.

Perhaps it was good that the night was no longer. In

the morning, when the sun streamed into the loft to announce 'wake-up' time, Blue Boy unthinkingly stretched as he did every morning and was surprised by the sudden pain that shot through him. He could not believe that one strenuous flight would make one feel so stiff and sore. He was used to long, daily exercise flights and should have felt very little soreness. He also wondered about the older birds who were not in shape like the younger ones.

Then he tipped his head and looked around the loft, watching the other birds as they awakened one by one.

Almost always as the birds awoke in the morning, they moved to stretch out some stiffness in their muscles from being in the same position while they slept. But on this morning, Blue Boy caught the same look of surprise and pain on their faces. They, too, were especially stiff and sore from the long flight the night before.

Out of respect to the leader of the flock, the birds stayed on their perches waiting for Goliath to make the first move to the feeding dishes. Goliath slept on.

Mrs. Goliath awoke, stretched—with pain showing in her eyes—looked at her husband and then at the flock as though to say to each one of them, "Don't you dare disturb him. The poor dear. Don't you dare."

Blue Boy waited and watched for Mrs. Malone to wake up. He was sure she would not let the stiff muscles go unannounced. He thought it unlikely too, that she could still her tongue and let the leader of the flock get more rest.

Mrs. Malone must have been exhausted by her flight. She was usually one of the first risers each morning, but today she continued sleeping. Blue Boy's stomach was complaining loudly. He could sense the restlessness in some of the other birds as well. How long could they wait before someone made a commotion?

Just when Blue Boy felt he wouldn't be able to stand it a moment longer, Mrs. Malone opened one eye, let it drift shut again, clicked her beak, and opened the eye again. Then with both eyes still half shut, she sleepily stretched out one wing. Blue Boy was sure she planned to follow by stretching out the other wing. Instead, her eyes popped wide open, and she groaned loudly.

With a look of sheer horror on her face she cried with a loud voice, "My wing—it's broken."

A soft chuckle rippled around the perches. Mrs. Malone didn't take too kindly to the laugh at her expense.

"You laugh," she screamed. "You laugh, and here I am suffering from a wing broken by fatigue."

Her screech awakened Goliath. He stirred slightly and frowned at the flock. Then his eyes fell on Molly Malone and he glared at her.

"My wing—and it's your fault. My wing is completely ruined. I'll never be able to fly again. Why I—."

"Hush," hissed Goliath. "Stop the uproar at once," and Goliath shifted upon his perch.

It was then that the stiffness of his muscles was made known to the big bird. Blue Boy saw him wince as the pain coursed through his body. Goliath tried to hide it, but the whole flock knew he was suffering.

It was Mrs. Goliath who saved the day again. In a calm, soft voice, she turned to the flock.

"Why don't the rest of you go on out to eat and exercise? I need a bit more sleep." She turned to Goliath. "Do you think you could wait awhile for breakfast, dear? I would love to catch a few more winks before the day gets too warm."

Goliath nodded and settled himself on the perch more comfortably.

"Mrs. Malone," said Mrs. Goliath, "I know you are hungry, my dear. Why don't you lead the way?"

"I doubt if I can even fly," complained Mrs. Malone. She was going to make a fuss, but Mrs. Goliath interrupted her. .

"Then hop down, dear," she said and gave her a brilliant smile.

Mrs. Malone walked along the perch until she came to the opening and then managed to make her sore wings work well enough to get down to the feed troughs. The rest of the flock followed.

Blue Boy wasn't surprised that the feed dishes were full. Didn't the man always have their breakfast waiting for them? Well, yesterday he had missed. But then yesterday had been an unusual day.

There was always some squabbling around the feed troughs—pecking and name-calling and little scraps—but this morning the usual scraps were heightened by the soreness of the birds. No one was in a good humor. All the birds objected when they were forced to use their muscles to hop away from another bird or escape the jab of a beak. And Molly Malone, having been given the privilege of leading the flock to the feeding dishes, decided to make the most of her foul mood and added authority. She pecked and chastised everyone who came within striking distance, until finally a wiry bird with a short temper took exception.

Blue Boy had seen it coming. Molly was just having too much fun throwing her weight around. She might consider herself the boss of the flock, but there were several flock members to whom she would need to prove her position.

Charlie Chaplin fed too close to Molly, to her way of thinking, and received a sharp peck as a result. He did not flutter away like the other flock members, but held his position—his eyes challenging Molly.

"Stop that," he threw at her. "If it's 'sport' you want, take that," and he pecked her on the neck—very hard.

For a moment Molly was taken aback. She had not expected to be challenged. She looked about to speak, then changed her mind, and with fire in her eyes, pecked Charlie again.

That was too much for Charlie. With wings slightly spread he propelled himself right at Molly, using both beak and feet to attack.

For a moment there was an awful fluttering of feathers as the two angry birds tore at one another—and then just as quickly, it was all over. It was Charlie Chaplin who had control of the feeding dish and Mrs. Malone retreated to a position at the edge of the flock, complaining loudly to herself and tending her wounds.

Blue Boy was much too busy eating to get concerned with the little tiff. The other pigeons ignored it, too; they were used to fights and squabbles. But inwardly, Blue Boy was glad Charlie had put Mrs. Malone in her proper place. It would make it that much easier for Goliath when he returned to the flock.

After they had their fill of breakfast, the flock used their stiff wings to propel them to the roof of the man's house. There they got a better look of the countryside than sitting on their loft.

It was another beautiful spring day—a good day for some exercise. Blue Boy hoped that it wouldn't be too long until they would be given the order to take a few laps. In the meantime, it was nice to sit in the sun and let its warm rays work the kinks out of his muscles.

He lay on his side and stretched out one wing lazily. Then he reversed and stretched the other. Already his wings were beginning to feel better. He was sure they would very quickly be just fine again.

In the neighbor's yard a door slammed. Then a voice called excitedly, "They're back! They're back!" Two pairs of feet ran to the fence separating the properties and two sets of eager eyes studied the pigeons on the roof.

The birds did not take to the air. They had seen the boys many times before, and as long as they stayed on their side of the fence, the birds did not object to their presence.

"Do you think they ate?"

"Sure they did—look at the troughs—they are nearly empty."

Two broad grins spread across two boyish faces—and then one of them seemed to freeze.

"Where's the big bird?"

"Who?"

"The big bird," said Timmie. "The leader."

Again two pairs of eyes carefully scanned the flock.

"He's not there. Neither is the smaller gray one who is always with him."

"Something must have happened to them."

"Boys," a voice called from the porch. "Get your jackets. It's time to leave for church."

The boys did not protest, but they explained excitedly.

"Mom, the big bird—the leader—and his mate— they're not with the flock."

"Maybe they are off somewhere else."

"But they always stay together."

"Maybe something happened to them, Mom."

Mrs. Thomas, too, looked troubled as she scanned the flock.

"I don't see them," she admitted. "We'll have to check as soon as we get home."

By the time the Thomases had returned from their

morning church service, Goliath and Mrs. Goliath had managed to get from the pen to the feeding dishes to have their breakfast. Then, because it was still difficult for Goliath to make his stiff wings work well, he fluttered to the house roof with a great deal of painful effort. He was content to sit basking in the sun with a few of the older members of the flock while the younger ones worked the kinks from their wings by exercise flights.

"He's here! He's here!" shouted Mark and Timmie in unison when they saw the big bird and his mate on the roof.

"Now a number of the other ones are gone," said Mrs. Thomas in exasperation.

"Oh, they're just exercising," Mark assured her. "Look—way over there by those trees. See them? They are just circling around to come back this way again."

Mrs. Thomas opened the door with her key and went to get their dinner on the table. She was glad the birds were all accounted for. It would make Mr. Faraday happy and certainly be a big relief to her two sons who took such pleasure in watching the birds.

Chapter Ten

Changes

That afternoon the Thomas family made a call at the local hospital to see how their neighbor, Mr. Faraday, was doing. The boys were a bit nervous about the visit. The thought of hospitals was frightening, and they had no idea how Mr. Faraday might feel about seeing them, even if they were caring for his pigeons. They took comfort in the presence of their mother and decided to let her lead the conversation.

This time the nurse did not try to prevent the boys from entering the old man's room. The doctor had left orders that they were to be allowed to see Mr. Faraday. He knew how important the pigeons were to Mr. Faraday and how much more quickly he would recover if assured that his pigeons were being well cared for. Besides, Doctor Conway had been drawn to the young boy, Timmie, who had looked at him with big brown eyes, pleading for the doctor to understand the dilemma of Mr. Faraday and his birds.

Mr. Faraday still looked weak and confused, but he was not the least bit hostile. The boys relaxed, and

Timmie thought the elderly man's eyes looked a bit brighter. Mr. Faraday still could not speak, so he needed to communicate by using a pencil and a sheet of paper.

"Divide into pens," wrote Mr. Faraday, "late."

The boys looked puzzled. They knew nothing about 'dividing' pigeons. They had thought that food and water was the only care pigeons needed.

"Medicine," wrote Mr. Faraday.

The boys' frowns deepened.

"Clarkson," wrote Mr. Faraday, and then followed it with a scrawled number.

All the pigeons had numbers—and even names. The boys had heard Mr. Faraday call his pigeons by name on occasion while he was working, and the boys were hidden behind the fence. The problem was, if they were hidden where they could hear Mr. Faraday, then they could not see him. And if they could see him, then they could not hear him. So when he called each pigeon by name, the boys had no idea which pigeon he was speaking to.

Now the boys looked at the name and the number on the sheet and were puzzled over it. Was Mr. Faraday trying to tell them of some specific pigeon who needed medicine?

They didn't want to upset Mr. Faraday by not understanding his message. What should they do? They looked to their mother. Her eyes seemed as worried as their own. She did not understand the message either.

Mr. Faraday could see he was not understood. He motioned for the paper once again and wrote down another word. "Fancier."

"Fancier. Fancier," repeated Mrs. Thomas, as she struggled to give meaning to the strange message.

A voice behind her spoke softly. "A 'fancier' is a

pigeon keeper."

Mrs. Thomas jumped slightly. She had not heard the man come in.

"I'm sorry," he apologized with a smile, "I didn't mean to startle you."

She smiled back. "I guess we were all so deeply absorbed in trying to decipher the message—."

"I'm Doctor Mike Conway," he offered, extending his hand. "I take it you are Mrs. Thomas."

She nodded.

Then he turned to the two boys. "Hello, Tim," he greeted Timmie. "And you must be brother Mark."

He shook hands with the boys too, and they felt grown-up and important.

"Mr. Faraday looks better today, don't you think, Tim?"

Timmie nodded, his eyes traveling to the face of the elderly man.

"Now, the message. Let's see if we can figure it out."

Mrs. Thomas handed Doctor Conway the sheet of paper with the scrawled words. He studied them one by one.

"Let's see. You want the birds divided into their pens—is that right?"

Mr. Faraday nodded.

"How are the boys to do that? Is there a special way to—?" but Mr. Faraday was waving his hand frantically in the air and pointing back at the paper.

The doctor looked down again.

"Clarkson," he read, and Mr. Faraday nodded his head wildly.

"Is Clarkson a pigeon?"

Mr. Faraday shook his head negatively.

"A man?"

Mr. Faraday nodded.

"I see," said the doctor. "Clarkson is a man who can separate the pigeons to the right pens. Is this his phone number then?"

Mr. Faraday nodded again, a look of relief in his eyes.

"Aha," said the doctor, "the riddle is solved. Mr. Clarkson, a pigeon fancier, whose number is given here, will come, if you call him, and care for the sorting of the pigeons."

Mr. Faraday managed a crooked smile of relief. It was the first time any of his next door neighbors had ever seen the old man smile.

Mrs. Thomas gave him a big smile in return and reached down and patted the feeble hand.

"We will call him the minute we get home," she promised. "Can he tell us all about the medicine, too?"

Mr. Faraday nodded.

"Everything?" continued Mrs. Thomas. "Can he tell us all we need to know about the pigeons?"

Mr. Faraday nodded again.

"Then we'll call him. We'll call him whenever we have a question."

Then Mrs. Thomas stopped and a frown crossed her face.

"What's wrong?" asked the doctor, noting her change of expression.

"Nothing much," she said, smiling again. "I just remembered that we'll have to call before we leave town. We don't have a phone."

Mr. Faraday signaled for the pencil and paper again, and with effort wrote across the sheet, "Use mine."

Mrs. Thomas nodded her agreement and then turned to her sons.

"I guess it's all settled then," she said, giving Mr. Faraday another smile. "We must go, boys. We don't want to tire Mr. Faraday."

Then she turned to Doctor Conway and gave him one of her special smiles.

"Thank you, Doctor, for your kindness," she said. "And for unscrambling our message for us."

"My pleasure," the doctor said, extending his hand, and from the light in his eyes, Mark thought that indeed he meant it.

Mr. Faraday signaled for the piece of paper one more time and scrawled across the empty space still on the bottom of the sheet, "Come again." With promises that indeed they would return, the three left the antiseptic-smelling room, feeling that it had been a good idea to call on their sick neighbor.

Chapter Eleven

Pigeons

It was all very strange to the pigeons. The man was still not around that day, but their food was there when they needed it. The water dish was filled with fresh water, as well. The flock had always supposed they only needed him to take care of their physical needs, but to their surprise, they found themselves wondering about him—missing him. They sat on the loft roof or on his house and watched and listened. When would he come? Where was he?

Mrs. Malone, who was still nursing her hurt feelings and her bruised wing from her scuffle with Charlie Chaplin earlier in the morning, sat meekly and quietly. She had been put in her proper place again, and she well knew it.

"It's very strange," commented Mrs. Goliath softly. "He has never left us like this before. Oh, maybe for an hour or two while he went off to get more feed—but overnight—and all day? Never."

Her husband shook his head as though he, too, could not understand it. He shifted his weight to ease his still aching body and frowned as he looked out over the yard. The man should be there. He should be there someplace.

Blue Boy, too, missed the man, but he was too young and carefree to worry about him for long. Besides, Blue Boy was busy studying the rest of the flock.

Not far from where he strutted back and forth along the peak of the roof, several of the young hens sat together twittering and cooing and making obvious eyes at their male counterparts. Blue Boy saw it all, though he pretended not to notice.

Something in the air told him it would soon be nesting time. Blue Boy had never nested before, being hatched near the end of the previous summer. None of the young hens who sat before him had nested either. Blue Boy knew that the mate one chose for nesting would be one's mate for life. He thought of Mighty Mouse, the mate of Molly Malone, and wondered how the poor fellow had been able to take her sharp tongue and the complaining for so many years.

Blue Boy shook his head and continued his pacing. He sure hoped he wouldn't meet the same fate as Mighty Mouse. Blue Boy had already been informed by Abner, an older friend in the flock, that he might not get to do his own choosing when it came to nesting time.

"The man often chooses," said Abner. "He pens the birds to produce the choicest offspring. Now our man, he wants fast birds—smart birds. He likes to win the meets. He thinks of strong bones and wing lengths and determination, things like that. He likes winners, our man does. He puts the trophies in his house on a shelf and sits and looks at them. I've seen them—through the window. And I've seen him—just sittin' there. Just sittin' there lookin' at them."

Blue Boy tried to dismiss the whole idea of nesting

from his mind. Just the same, it was difficult to give it no thought at all when the spring sun shone upon the ground causing flowers and grass to consider rousing themselves from their winter beds, and the soft warm breeze seemed to whisper that the world was a good place to be. The birds they hadn't seen all winter were now singing in the budding limbs of the trees or rushing about building nests.

And then Blue Boy overheard a conversation.

Two of the older pigeons sat close together on the rooftop talking in low tones.

"I wonder where the man went?" asked the hen.

"I've no idea," said the cock. "It is a strange time for him just to disappear."

"Strange time?"

"Nesting time. Can't you just feel it—all around us? See—those birds right over there are building their nest—and over there near the pond—see the ducks?"

"What if he doesn't come back? Will we need to build in the open, too?"

"I don't know. We've never had to build our own nest before. Would you know how to begin? I'm afraid I wouldn't know a thing about it."

"We'd just have to try, I guess."

Blue Boy moved on, sorry to have been eavesdropping, but the conversation made him even more uneasy. What would they all do if the man did not return? Would the new squabs be safe from predators?

Blue Boy cast his eyes around the flock, deciding to play a little game with himself.

"If the man does not come back—and I have to choose my own mate," he asked himself, "who would I choose?"

There were many very attractive young hens in the flock. Blue Boy let his eyes travel over them. For one

reason or another he discarded them one by one, until he was down to three very pretty birds.

"Wow!" he thought, "it really would be hard to decide. *She* has beautiful markings, but *she* has such long sleek wing feathers. And *she*—." Just as Blue Boy was summing up the merits of the third young hen, she caught him looking her way and gave him just the hint of a smile. Blue Boy felt his heart leap within his breast. He turned quickly to hide his self-consciousness, but somehow knew that he hadn't turned quickly enough. Surely she had seen his embarrassment.

With more strut to his stride, he worked his way back across the peak of the roof and settled down to soak up some sun. But he couldn't help but steal a glimpse in the direction of the young hen now and then—and once or twice, he thought she might have been stealing a few glances at him as well.

Chapter Twelve

Healing

As soon as Mr. Clarkson heard the news concerning Mr. Faraday, he made a hospital visit to his fellow fancier. He got all the proper instructions about the birds and then came directly to the acreage. Mr. Clarkson had handled pigeons for many years and understood exactly what was to be done.

Mark and Timmie watched carefully. They wanted to learn all they could about handling the birds. First, the birds were separated into the proper pens. The pairs of pigeons were placed in their own little compartments so that they could set up housekeeping. They would be busy all summer long raising new youngsters to join the flock. As many as three hatchings per summer would keep both the hen and cock very busy caring for and feeding the babies.

If the bird-handler had been watching carefully, he might have caught the gleam in the eye of Blue Boy as he was selected to share a nest with the pretty young bird that he had flirted with on the rooftop. Her name was Lady Jane, and she was a beautiful bird—both in dress and in disposition.

No father was ever more excited than Blue Boy when the first squab freed himself from the shell and made his noisy and demanding appearance. Soon a somewhat smaller bird joined him. The two little ones were named Blue Boy the Second and Annabelle by the boys who cared for them.

All spring long the birds had to be watched carefully for disease. Medications were given systematically to prevent illness from overtaking the flock. Following Mr. Clarkson's instructions, Mark and Timmie soon learned just how to add medication to the feed or water.

Mr. Clarkson also showed the boys how to handle the birds properly—feeling the wings and body for strength and fullness—and how to regulate the exercise programs of the various birds.

Doctor Conway also became interested in the pigeons and looked for books written by fanciers so that the boys might read and understand all they could about the birds.

Mr. Faraday improved. It seemed terribly slow at first, but then the healing process took place much more quickly.

After several weeks, he was allowed to come home, even though he was unable to walk about his acreage like he had been used to. School was now out for the summer, and the boys were able to be nearby if Mr. Faraday needed them. The boys had thought that once Mr. Faraday was able to care for the birds on his own, he would send them back to their own yard again. They hated to think of going back to the old relationship with their neighbor.

But it was not so. Even after Mr. Faraday began to hobble about with his cane, he still seemed to expect the boys' daily visit. Gone was the grouchy neighbor they had known when they first moved into the rented house. Instead, the old man seemed to enjoy the company of the two young boys almost as much as he enjoyed their helping hands.

Mr. Faraday spent much of his time sitting on the porch and watching the birds and the boys. On occasion, Mr. Clarkson would also join him, and the two men would talk 'pigeons' while the two boys listened intently with eyes fixed on their faces. Pigeons were their delight, and the talk of pigeons was absolutely fascinating. They had learned to love the birds dearly and now knew each of the flock by name and number.

Mr. Faraday could talk much better now, and one day as he and the boys sat upon the porch sipping lemonade that Mrs. Thomas had made, he surprised them with an exciting suggestion.

"I've watched you fellas work with the birds for some time now, and it seems to me that you are first-rate 'fanciers.' It's about time you had a loft of your own."

"We could never afford one," Mark said realistically. "It's all Mom can do to pay the rent and buy the groceries."

"Yeah," agreed Timmie. "Good birds cost lots of money—an' I wouldn't want just any old birds."

A twinkle showed in Mr. Faraday's eyes.

"You like good birds, huh?" he grunted.

"Yeah," said both boys at once.

"You think I have good birds?" continued Mr. Faraday.

He knew the answer to that one. The boys loved his birds—and well, they should. Mr. Faraday had registered birds. He had the best. That was why he was so careful to see that they got only the best feed, the best exercise program, and the best handling. He had several trophies on his mantle to prove that his birds were the best, and other 'fanciers' were always trying to talk Mr. Faraday into selling one of his top birds.

"Yeah," said the boys, "the best."

"Well, I agree with you on that one," chuckled Mr. Faraday. "Now, if I was to tell you that you can pick a squab—any squab from the loft—which one would you pick?"

The boys thought that Mr. Faraday was playing a little game with them.

"That's easy," said Mark. "I'd pick Blue Boy the Second."

"And you?" asked Mr. Faraday, turning to Timmie.

"I would, too," said Timmie. "He's gonna be the prettiest, and the fastest—and I think he's the smartest, too."

"You do, eh?" said Mr. Faraday, with another chuckle. "Well, you are even better fanciers than I thought. You are right, and I'd pick Blue Boy the Second, too." Then Mr. Faraday chuckled again, "You little rascals," he laughed, "You just beat me out of my best bird."

The boys just looked at the old man.

"So how do you plan to care for your pigeons?" said the senior fancier. "You need a loft you know."

"What do you mean?" asked Timmie innocently.

"I mean—I gave you a pair of birds—Blue Boy and— of course that means a little hen comes with him. We will pick the hen out together. She must be a good match."

"But—but—."

"No buts—they are your responsibility now. You need a loft."

Timmie threw his arms around Mr. Faraday's neck, the tears streaming down his face. To say 'thank-you' seemed so inadequate. Mark, followed the lead of his younger brother. He had been going to shake hands with the old man and express his thanks as sincerely as he knew how, but when he saw that Mr. Faraday did not seem to object to Timmie's hug, a hug seemed the proper thing to do.

Mr. Faraday wiped away a few tears of his own as he watched the two boys run excitedly home, hardly able to comprehend their good news. Mrs. Thomas could hear them coming long before they ever reached the back door.

"We've got pigeons! We've got pigeons! Our very own! Our very own pigeons!"

When the boys phoned the doctor to tell him their good news, he volunteered to help them with building the new loft for their birds.

In the warm summer days that followed, and under the careful eye of Mr. Faraday, the loft was built. It had been a time of fun and sharing. Never had Mark and Timmie felt happier.

Mr. Faraday was now a good friend. It was almost like having a grandfather. And Doctor Mike was more than a doctor. He was a friend—and a partner—and good company for all of them. He knew how to do lots of things and was often there when the boys wanted to play catch or learn how to spin a top—or build a loft. They didn't know how they would have managed building the loft without his help.

But the boys also noticed, though they didn't talk about it, that their mother seemed to enjoy the company of Dr. Mike, too. In fact, the two of them seemed to spend a lot of time just 'visiting.'

When the loft was all finished, they stood back to admire it.

"I'll go get Mr. Faraday," volunteered Mark. "He

will want to give it one last inspection.''

Mr. Faraday beamed as he looked over the loft.

''Good work,'' he said over and over. ''It's a first-class loft for first-class birds.'' Then he grinned teasingly at Dr. Mike, ''Good work—for a doctor.''

''When can we move them?'' asked Mark and Timmie in unison.

''Give them another week,'' said Mr. Faraday.

The boys cheered and jumped up and down.

''Don't forget that you need to get your food supply and your medicine all lined up, too,'' Mr. Faraday reminded them. The boys agreed that they still had some work to do.

But the time was heavy on the boys' hands. They so much wanted their own birds—and could hardly wait for the week to go by so that they could move the young squabs.

''I know,'' said Mark one morning when they were looking for something to make the time go more quickly. ''The loft looks so bare. Mr. Faraday's is a nice blue-gray color. Ours should be painted, too. Let's paint it.''

''Where will we get the paint?'' asked Timmie.

''Mr. Engleson does painting for folks. Maybe he has some left over. Let's ask him.''

And so the boys hopped on their bikes and rode down the road to see Mr. Engleson. He was happy to give them any paint they needed from his leftovers, so the boys started sifting through the cans for a nice color.

''None of it will do the whole loft,'' said Timmie, shaking each can.

Mark stopped—but for only a minute. ''That won't matter,'' he insisted. ''Let's make it even prettier. We can paint the loft a whole bunch of nice colors.''

With old discarded brushes, also from their friend, Mr. Engleson, the boys set to work. All afternoon they painted—coloring one section a bright orange, a door red, another section green, then one blue. They added bits of pink to the peak, some chocolate brown to some perches, and trimmed it all with a nice pale yellow.

To them it looked 'just right.' Bright and personal. Their very own loft.

"It looks great," said Timmie. "Mom will like it, too. Bet there's no other loft anywhere as pretty or as colorful as ours."

Their loft was colorful alright. Though some folks might have questioned the 'pretty' part, the two boys beamed with pride.

In just two days they would get their own birds. They could hardly wait. That night they poured over the 'pigeon' books again.

"Did you know that in some places, they call lofts 'cotes'?" asked Mark of Timmie.

Timmie looked up in surprise; he had never heard that. Mrs. Thomas made a comment from the chair where she sat mending the knee of a small pair of blue jeans.

"I thought cotes were for sheep," she said.

"That's right—sheep or pigeons. They call both of them cotes."

"Why don't we call our loft a cote?" asked Timmie.

"Cause—here in our country, they call them lofts."

"That doesn't mean we have to," insisted Timmie. "We painted ours different. We can call it different, too, if we want to."

To Mark it made perfect sense.

"Let's," he said. "Mr. Faraday's will be the *loft*. Ours will be the *cote*. Then we will never get mixed up about which one we are talking about."

Timmie grinned. He liked the idea very much. Now they had their very own cote—and a very colorful cote it was, too.

Mrs. Thomas smiled. Then she giggled softly. Two pairs of eyes looked at her questioningly.

"I was just thinking," she said with the laugh that was bubbling up within her, "your cote—it's a cote of many colors."

The two boys joined in her laughter.

Chapter Thirteen

Fanciers

Blue Boy the Second remembered very little about the day he changed homes. At the time, it was a frightening experience for him, but all of the squabs found the leaving of their nest rather frightening.

For Blue Boy the Second, it meant not only leaving the safety of the nest and the care of devoted parents, but changing to a new loft as well. Well, not even a loft, a 'cote'—a colorful cote that still smelled rather badly from its coat of fresh paint.

If Mr. Faraday worried about the paint smell, he did not mention it to the boys. They were so excited, all they could think about was their fancy cote and their new birds.

To join Blue Boy the Second, so he wouldn't be lonely in his new surroundings, a young squab by the name of Josie was also to be transferred to the new pen. Josie was a bit smaller than Blue Boy the Second, but she seemed strong and energetic. Mr. Faraday was sure she would make a good nesting mate for Blue Boy the Second when that time arrived.

The squabs were quite aware of all the fuss and drew back as far from the reaching hands as possible. They weren't able to escape them, however, and soon were lifted carefully from the nests and held firmly, yet gently, in a pair of strong hands.

Mr. Faraday scrutinized each bird carefully before handing them over to their proud new owners. Then he walked to the next yard with Mark and Timmie to help get the birds settled into their new surroundings.

At first, the young female was frightened by it all and cowered in the corner, refusing to touch the water or food that was offered. Blue Boy the Second was a bit more brave and soon bold enough to explore their new home.

They certainly had enough room—and all to themselves, too. Blue Boy the Second liked having room to feed alone at the dish and room to test his newly forming wing feathers.

The three bystanders stood watching from a distance that would not intimidate the birds.

"Do you think they like it?" asked Timmie.

"I'm sure they will," assured Mr. Faraday. "Why, I'll bet there isn't another 'cote' like this one anywhere in the country."

Mark beamed.

"I hope they'll be happy." Timmie went on wistfully. "Will they miss their mom and dad?"

"Oh, sure they will," said Mr. Faraday. "They had good moms and dads who took good care of them. But everyone has to grow up. All the other squabs their age are going to be moved away from their moms and dads, too. I'm going to be doing that in the next few days. They will all be upset for a little while—but they soon adjust."

"What's 'adjust'?" asked Timmie.

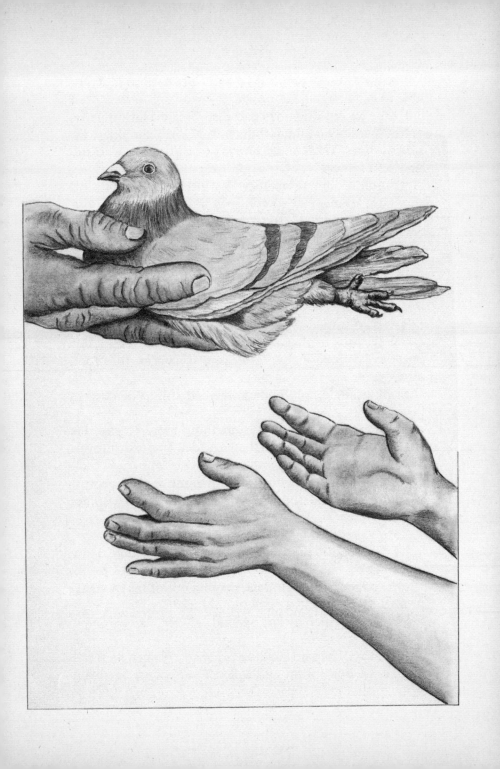

"Adjust? Well, adjust is to—to—get used to it. To be able to get along on your own."

"Like we did when our dad died," said Mark quietly.

Mr. Faraday let a hand drop to Mark's shoulder. He said nothing. What could one say to a little boy who still needed a father?

"I don't even remember," whispered Timmie. "I don't even remember what he was like anymore."

The conversation was getting a bit difficult for Mr. Faraday to handle. He said in a voice that was a bit too loud, a bit too forceful, "The squabs won't remember either. In a day or two they will have forgotten all about living with their parents. They will be happy to be on their own."

The boys turned their thoughts back to the birds.

"Well, look at that Blue Boy the Second," said Mr. Faraday, "there he is a-picking away at the food already."

Mark grinned, but Timmie seemed still to be deep in thought.

Mr. Faraday fought for something more to say. He couldn't think of much—then an idea popped into his head.

"Blue Boy the Second is a long name for a pigeon," he said. "Do you suppose you should call him something different?"

"He's already registered," said Mark.

"That doesn't matter. You can call him any name you want to.

"Let's then," said Timmie, coming out of his thoughtfulness. "What shall we call him, Mark?"

"We could call him The Second."

Timmie grinned.

"No way," he said shaking his head. "When he starts to race, we don't want him called The Second. We want him to be The First, don't we, Mr. Faraday?"

Mr. Faraday began to laugh.

"You bet you do," he said. "You bet you do."

And then Mr. Faraday thought of his own mantle and the trophy cups he had been collecting. Would the day come when one of the boys' birds would take away a cup that he coveted?

"They well could," he admitted to himself. "They very well could." Mr. Faraday knew that the pigeon the boys had picked was the best squab in the lot. He grinned to himself. Somehow the losing of a cup to the boys didn't seem so bad.

The next months were spent caring for the birds. The boys had settled on the name of Blue for the young cock. When his longer wing feathers grew in, he was even more impressive than he had been as a squab. His little nest mate grew strong and agile as well, and soon the two birds were released for flying exercises.

The first time the boys allowed them to fly off from the cote, they both stood holding their breath. What if they didn't come back? What if they returned to their old home next door? What if they got lost? And the worst fear of all, what if a hawk got them?

The hawk was the most dreaded enemy of the flyer. Many good birds had gone down by the claws of a hawk. Hunters—men with guns—also claimed a number of homers every year, and there were even those with their trained hunting birds—hawks or falcons—who took the lives of several homers every season.

The boys read about the enemies of their birds. They read with fear and trembling. There was no way the boys could protect their birds once they were in flight. They had to trust them to their instincts and their flying ability.

So it was with great relief that Mark and Timmie saw their beloved birds circling around over the acreage before coming back into the cote.

Mr. Faraday had been watching the birds as well. As a seasoned fancier, he felt he had seen few birds with such promise as the young Blue. He flew with a lightness and grace that made him beautiful to watch, and from handling him, the old man knew his wing bones were finely tuned and strong.

Yes, he should do very well. Very well. Barring accidents or injuries, the young cock looked like he might make an excellent candidate for racing.

Mr. Faraday was anxious to get back to the training of his own birds. He had lost a whole racing season because of the stroke. His birds weren't back in racing form yet; but hopefully, with the help of his two young neighbors, he'd get them back in shape again—perhaps in time for some of the shorter spring meets. Maybe the boys would have Blue ready for a few test races, as well.

Mr. Faraday smiled to himself. It was nice to feel like sort of a 'team.' He had missed companionship, even though he would have hotly denied it. Still, one did need more than birds to communicate with. He thoroughly enjoyed the boys. It would have been his loss if he had gone on barring them from his yard. Perhaps the stroke —the pesky thing—had done him a favor after all.

Chapter Fourteen

Training

Blue stood on the cote roof looking out over the acreage that he regarded as home. He had flown farther and longer this morning than he had ever done before. Yes, he felt good. Hardly winded. He looked down at the bird beside him. Her sleek sides were raising slightly —up and down—up and down. The flying had been a bit harder for her than it had for him. Yet, he felt exhilarated—like he was ready to go for several more laps around the countryside. He was tempted to take to the air again, but he knew she was tired and would feel obliged to follow.

From next door Blue could hear loud, angry voices of a disagreement. It was not uncommon for the flock to be arguing. Blue had heard rumors that the old bird, Goliath, was getting past his prime and no longer able to give the strong leadership the flock needed. Because of this fact, a number of the younger cocks were vying for the position. Blue hoped the issue would soon be settled so there might be some peace and quiet in the neighborhood.

Suddenly, without warning, there was a great commotion next door. Blue craned his neck to try to see what had caused the disturbance, but he could see nothing. Nothing, that is, except big bird Goliath urging the flock to take refuge quickly within the loft.

Blue craned his neck further, stretching it to the limit. Was the old bird using this as some strange tactic to show that he was still in command?

Soon all was deathly quiet.

Josie, Blue's flying mate, had been quietly preening her feathers. She had seemingly paid little attention to the fuss from the next yard. Blue reasoned that there wasn't one nosey bone in all of Josie's body. She never seemed to pay attention to the bickering or vying for position that would have interested most birds.

Blue admired that—and at the same time he was intrigued by her lack of curiosity.

"Goliath is still calling the orders," he informed her.

She blinked her eyes slightly and straightened another shining feather.

"Does the noise bother you?" he went on, seeking to get some response from the young hen.

"What noise?" she asked demurely. "It's deathly quiet."

Something about her strange choice of words jerked Blue's eyes from the yard next door and toward the skies. He should have suspected it sooner. He just hadn't thought. There, swooping silently toward them, and closing the gap swifter than he would have thought imaginable, was the largest hawk that Blue had ever seen.

He only had time to scream, "Hawk!" before making his dash for the cover of the cote.

With a bone-chilling screech, Josie rose to join him. Before Josie could lift herself into the air for proper

flight, the hawk was almost upon her. Her lunge forward evaded the out-thrust claws of the big bird, but his strong wing hit her on the back, sending her crashing to the ground—rolling over and over as she fell.

The hawk would have most assuredly returned to pick up its victim had not the screen door banged as Mark came running out to see what had startled his birds.

Instead of returning for his prey, the hawk, with an angry cry, rose into the air and circled back toward the distant forests.

Poor little Josie. She was too shaken up even to right herself on her feet. Her wing hung at a crooked angle, and her eyes blinked in confusion.

Mark picked her up tenderly and stroked her soft back feathers as he talked to her. Eventually, the thumping of her little heart slowed down, and Mark carried her to the house. Timmie was immediately dispatched for Mr. Faraday, and Mark put in an urgent call to the hospital to page Dr. Mike.

"She's hurt really bad," Mark cried over the phone, and Dr. Mike promised to have someone cover for him so that he could come immediately. He wasn't sure he could help the bird—but he might be able to be of some help to the boys.

Josie's wing had been broken. Blue felt it was all his fault. He had known about hawks and should have had his wits about him. He must remember to keep one eye on the sky at all times.

Josie was tenderly cared for while her wing was healing, and Blue was given another flying partner so his training would not be interrupted.

The new bird was a strong young cock. He was a bit older than Blue and loved to boast of his strength and his speed. This irked Blue somewhat, and every day he pushed himself to be just a little bit faster—and go a little bit farther. Mr. Faraday who watched on, decided that they had done just the right thing. Blue was quickly developing into a marvelous flyer. And he would be a more cautious bird, as well. At the expense of poor little Josie, Blue had learned firsthand the dangers of the enemy, the hawk. He was sure to fly now with more care and concern.

Though Blue did not forget his lesson on hawks, he still could not totally ignore the goings-on next door. He was interested in old Goliath and hated to see the big bird lose control of the flock.

It wouldn't be a hen who would take over the leadership—even though Molly Malone was the most vocal of the flock members. No, it would be another cock who would lead the flock. Each member of the flock knew that—and so did Molly. But she said her piece, complained about the leadership, and picked on the other hens and younger birds just for the sport of it.

The nesting season had ended for another year, and the boys were busy back in school. They were spending their free time caring for their birds and pouring over 'pigeon' books provided by the kind doctor. Josie's wing was almost back to normal.

Winter was coming. One could feel the nip in the air. The birds took to the sky frequently, partly because they loved to fly, but also because it kept the blood swiftly coursing through their narrow veins.

Blue was gaining strength and ability daily. He didn't fly often with the flock, but on occasion he could not resist lifting into the air when he saw them off for a morning exercise. He wanted to be able to compare his speed with that of other birds. Though the young cock was a good exercise mate, Blue wanted to know just where he would stand with the rest of the flock.

Josie was only allowed short flights, as yet, and then

was penned again. Blue knew he needed far more exercise than that. When he flew with Josie, he flew much more slowly, giving consideration to her healing wing. But when he flew with the other birds, he loved to see if he could beat them. At times he would even purposely drop behind and then put on a burst of speed to see how quickly he could catch them again.

Flying was not a chore for Blue. It was a passion. He loved the feeling of the cold air filling his lungs. He loved the feeling of the earth passing swiftly beneath him. He loved the sport of pursuit, the energy that came from energy expended. Some days he felt he could just fly on and on forever. He wondered where it would take him if he just lifted his blue barred wings and headed for the distant horizon without ever looking back.

But Blue was a 'homer.' As soon as he lifted himself aloft, there was that something within him that pulled him back toward his own loft—his crazy-colored cote. It was there—like an unseen tether, pulling and urging him to return home. And Blue always obeyed the voice from deep within him. It could not be denied. No matter what the horizon promised—there was always the stronger pull to circle for home.

Chapter Fifteen

The Race

The next few months were spent getting the birds into top racing form. Mark and Timmie rushed home from school each day to get their orders from Mr. Faraday. He advised the boys on what should be done with Blue to help him develop. Blue's feed was mixed with utmost care, and a strict ration given to him each morning. His medications were administered with equal attention.

Mr. Faraday watched his wing feathers and checked his weight. He tested his strength and endurance with practice flights. Mark and Timmie watched it all with eager eyes. They were given the opportunity to compare Blue with Mr. Faraday's choice birds, and they beamed when they realized they had picked a possible winner.

Mr. Faraday brought them the Racing News, and Mark and Timmie circled three dates in red ink, hoping that by then Blue would be ready to try his first races.

Three weeks before the first date, Mr. Faraday paid a visit to the boys' cote. He handled Blue, feeling his bone structure, his weight, his flexibility. He studied his eyes, his feathers, his feet and beak. Then he set him loose to fly free-form around the acreage, watching carefully as he circled, soared and came in to land.

"Do you think he'll be ready?" asked Timmie anxiously.

Mr. Faraday smiled. "He's ready," he answered, "and if I know anything about pigeons, he'll be the one to beat by this time next year."

Mark grinned. He knew that a young bird had much to learn about racing. Mr. Faraday had told the boys not to expect too much the first few races.

"Guess we'd better get you fellas signed up in the Club," continued Mr. Faraday. "You've got to be a member in order to race your bird. And you're gonna need your own time clock, too."

Soon the formalities were taken care of, and the boys became the holders of an official club membership. Their mother framed the document and put in on their bedroom wall.

A few days later when Mr. Faraday came over to see the boys, he had some further instructions.

"Time to get your registration in for the first race," he informed them, and the registration was taken care of.

The first race came nearer and nearer. Dr. Mike promised to drive all of them over to the location where the birds were to be gathered for shipping.

The first race was only 100 miles and acted as a trial run for the young birds. Mark and Timmie both knew that Blue was capable of handling such a flight with no problem, but still when the day of the race arrived, both boys were nervous.

"I've got a tummy ache," complained Timmie. "I think I'm getting something."

Mark put a hand to Timmie's head. "You don't feel hot," he offered.

"Well, I feel sick. Maybe we shouldn't let Blue fly. He might feel sick, too."

"I'm sure that Blue is just fine," said Dr. Mike, "but just in case, we'll let Mr. Faraday take one last look at him." Then he took Timmie's hand and lead him to his car. "And I have something for you, son, that might help your tummy a bit."

Timmie took the offered pill and it did settle his stomach. Still he felt nervous about Blue, even after Mr. Faraday assured them that Blue was in top form.

Blue was placed carefully in his special carrier. The family then hopped into Dr. Mike's car and drove to the stated location. Mr. Faraday and his four racers followed them in Mr. Faraday's old Chevy. Mrs. Thomas had packed a picnic lunch for all of them so they could celebrate the day of the first race, but she secretly wondered just how much of the lunch would be eaten. Everyone was far too excited to think about food.

As Dr. Mike pulled his car alongside a red station wagon and turned off the engine, Mark could feel chills go all up his spine. Timmie put a hand on his complaining stomach. It felt much better, but he still was all squishy inside.

Mark lifted the bird carrier from the car, and they stood and waited while Mr. Faraday parked the Chevy and got out to remove his birds. Then they all went together to have the birds checked into the race.

Blue knew something very out-of-the-ordinary was about to happen. He had made little trips in the bird carrier before and been taken short distances from home. Then he was set free to test his ability to find his way home on his own. Blue had enjoyed the adventures. But today—today was something different—he could sense it. There was an air of excitement all around him. He could even sense the uneasiness in the way that his humans handled him.

After all the birds were checked, the crowd of fanciers were given one more review of the racing rules. Then their watches were all set in exact synchronization so that they could double-check their time clocks when they got home. The trucks carrying the birds pulled away from the parking lot.

Timmie reached for Mark's hand, and the two brothers watched the cargo of birds disappear down the street.

"I wish he wasn't a homer," whispered Timmie. "I wish he was just a bird."

Mark agreed with Timmie at the moment—but at the same time he felt a good deal of pride in the bird they had just bid farewell.

"Well," said Mrs. Thomas cheerfully, "let's go have our picnic."

"We need to get home," said Mark. "We want to be there when Blue gets back."

"Mark," said his mother, "they aren't even going to release the birds until six o'clock in the morning. It is only five o'clock in the afternoon. We have lots of time for a picnic."

Mark knew she was right, but it still didn't seem right that no one was at home to greet Blue. And he would be coming—sometime, he would be coming.

Reluctantly, the boys crawled back into Dr. Mike's car. They drove down to the river and pulled up near the bank.

"Anybody for fishing?" called Dr. Mike, just as Mr. Faraday pulled up beside them.

The boys just shook their heads, but Mr. Faraday accepted one of the rods.

It seemed to take their mother forever to spread out the picnic. It wasn't that they were hungry, they just wanted to get the formality of eating over with so that they could go home and watch the cote.

While Mrs. Thomas gathered the remains of the picnic, Mr. Faraday went back to his fishing and Dr. Mike suggested throwing a football. Mark and Timmie tried to act enthused, but it was difficult. Finally, Dr. Mike tossed the ball back in the car and went to help Mrs. Thomas pack up the leftovers.

Mark wandered down to the stream and sat on a rock beside Mr. Faraday. He said nothing, but his eyes were troubled. Soon Timmie joined them and claimed another rock.

Silence hung heavily over them for a few moments. Finally, Mr. Faraday broke it.

"I remember when I sent off my first cock," he said, as he tossed his baited hook back into the water. "It was scary. His name was Georgie Boy and he was beautiful. I knew that I might never see him again."

At the boys' looks of horror, Mr. Faraday went on, "Oh, he was in perfect condition, I had seen to that. But I knew the risks. Lots of things out there to stop a bird from coming home. One has to think about those things."

There was another pause as Mr. Faraday reeled in the line.

"He made it, though. Oh, he didn't win. He didn't even make good time. But he made it. I was never so glad to see a bird come in as I was Georgie Boy."

"You think Blue will make it?" whispered Mark.

"He's strong," said Mr. Faraday. "An' he's smart. An' he sure can fly. I think that he's got a real good chance of being in the top twenty."

Just hearing Mr. Faraday say it, helped a little.

They went home then, and the boys tried to keep their minds busy until bedtime. It was hard. They spent some time out at the cote talking to a lonesome Josie. She had never been kept apart from Blue overnight before. Mark feared that she, too, would get no sleep.

Bedtime came. The boys brushed their teeth, put on their pajamas, and said their prayers. Even after praying for Blue, they still couldn't dismiss him from their minds—though it had helped.

Mark thought the next morning would never come. He was up early and out to the cote. Timmie soon joined him.

"Couldn't you sleep either?" asked Mark.

Timmie shook his head.

"Has he started yet?" he asked sleepily.

Mark consulted the clock.

"About five minutes ago," he answered.

Timmie's face lit up. "Then he's on his way," he smiled. "He'll be home before we know it."

But the morning dragged by very slowly. The boys tried to keep their minds busy by reviewing the rules.

"Now when he gets here," said Mark, "we need to let him go in his pen. Then we go in, catch him, take off his band and punch it in the time clock."

"Right," said Timmie.

"I hope nothing scares him, so he'll go right to the pen," went on Mark.

"Me, too," said Timmie, but as time went on Timmie had a change of heart.

Their eyes were sore from straining to catch a glimpse of a bird against the brightness of the sky. More than once they had run to the edge of the property and peered eagerly westward, but still no bird had come into sight. Once Timmie thought that he had seen him coming, but it had turned out to be a passing bluejay. In disappointment he took up his station again.

"Mark," he said soberly. "I don't really care if Blue

hurries into the pen or not. I just want him to get home again.''

Mark nodded slowly. The important thing was for Blue to return safely.

And then they saw a small fleck in the sky, and they watched as it grew bigger and bigger. It was a bird. And it was heading straight for their property. As it came closer they could see that it was a pigeon. They were about to cheer loudly when they noticed that the bird did not fly like Blue. It was one of Mr. Faraday's four entries.

Another of Mr. Faraday's birds returned before Blue made his appearance. By then, the boys had forgotten the competition. They were so glad to see their Blue arrive safely that they thought of nothing else.

It was long after Blue had landed, returned to the pen, and helped himself to some much deserved rations, that the boys thought of the band and the time clock.

"Hey," shouted Mark, "we forgot to time him."

"Who cares," said Timmie. "He's home. That's what matters.''

Chapter Sixteen

Excitement

Blue was entered in several more small races. It became much easier for the boys to let him go, and they even enjoyed the excitement of watching the skies for the returning homer. They did not forget to pen and clock him again. His times were getting better, and Mr. Faraday was beaming everytime he knew the young cock's time.

Blue had already tallied three thirds, two fourths, and a tenth place when Mr. Faraday prompted the boys to enter him in one of the bigger races. The race was 2,500 miles, and a large purse, in the boys' thinking, was at stake.

At night they would lie in their bunks and whisper about what they would do with the money if they won. They discussed new red bikes with balloon tires, a football just like the one Dr. Mike brought with him, a new T.V. so the picture wouldn't keep jumping, and all sorts of other things.

They talked about things for their mom, too. In fact, that is what they talked about most of all. A new handbag—she was embarrassed about the frayed straps on her old one, a new coat for church, and a new clock in her kitchen so she wouldn't need to keep moving the hands forward five minutes every day.

They even talked about what they would like to get for Mr. Faraday and Dr. Mike. That prize money from the race could bring to them many things that would provide happiness.

But mostly they talked about Blue. Already his name was becoming known in racing circles. Other fanciers, with bigger operations than the boys', had their eyes on the slim, blue bird. They even had an offer from one loft. The man said they could pick any two young cocks from his loft, and he would add one hundred dollars, in exchange for the young Blue. If the boys hadn't loved Blue so, the offer might have been tempting. As it was, they wouldn't consider selling Blue for any price.

But if—if they could keep Blue—and have money, too—prize money—then everything would be just perfect. The boys found themselves looking forward to the 'big' race with wild anticipation.

"Mark," asked Timmie, "do you think that Mom would be able to quit work and stay home with us if Blue won first prize?"

"First prize? Blue has never been first yet—and he'll be racing against all the best homers this time. First prize? Mr. Faraday said maybe fourth to sixth. Remember?"

Timmie was quiet for a moment.

"Bet he could win first prize if he really wanted to. He's really fast, Mark. When he wants to fly fast, he leaves all the other birds way behind. I've seen him."

"I know he's fast—but—you need more than fast— you need—you need drive—that's what Mr. Faraday says."

"Don't you think that Blue has drive?"

"I dunno. Mr. Faraday thinks that so far Blue has just been flying for fun. He thinks he could be faster if he really wanted to."

Timmie thought about that.

"What gives 'em drive?"

"I don't know. Nobody really knows why they come back at all. Or how they find their way either."

"I think he comes home to Josie," said Timmie, "Josie—and the cote. He knows the cote is his home."

"Mr. Faraday says that he might fly faster if he had squabs in the nest. He would know Josie needs his help to take care of them."

"The eggs won't be hatched by then—I just know it. Remember we marked the calendar—they still need six more days until they hatch. Blue has to be shipped on Wednesday."

"Mr. Faraday was talking with Dr. Mike and he said he might switch eggs with one of his hens and then they would hatch sooner."

"He did? I never heard that."

"I don't think I was s'pose to hear it either," said Timmie in an apologetic whisper. "They didn't know I was behind them."

"Is that fair?" asked Mark.

"I dunno. They aren't helping the bird fly—just making him want to fly faster. He still has to do all the work himself."

"I dunno," said Mark. "It sounds like it isn't fair."

"Mr. Faraday says fanciers have lots of ways to get the birds to come home faster. They—."

"Boys," came a call from the kitchen, "it's time you were sleeping. Save the chatter for tomorrow."

With a "Yes, Mom," the boys snuggled down under

their blankets and tried to go to sleep. It was not easy for either of them. Their thoughts were still on racing pigeons, hatching eggs, and new kitchen clocks.

If Blue could win first prize, would it really be possible for Mrs. Thomas to stay home? It sure would be nice.

The next day when Mark and Timmie went to care for Blue and Josie, two featherless squabs were pushing their way from the shells that had confined them. Blue was proud and excited. It was his and Josie's first hatching.

Mark looked at Timmie and Timmie look at Mark. The knowledge that Mr. Faraday had hurried the process somewhat dampened the excitement of the first hatching for the boys, but seeing the way Blue strutted and cooed made them laugh in spite of it all.

Blue was all business that day. He couldn't even be tempted out for an exercise flight. Mark worried about it, but Mr. Faraday, when he was consulted, said there was no need to worry. Mr. Faraday was more concerned that there would be a strong bonding between Blue and the new squabs in the two days left before his shipping.

The next morning Blue was still fussing over the two new members of his family; he did take his morning exercise flight—though he cut it short to get back to Josie and the two babies. Josie then took her turn while Blue cared for their young.

And then it was the day for the shipping. Mark and Timmie rode with their mom and Dr. Mike to the airport. This time the birds were going by plane to the starting point so they wouldn't need to be confined for the long drive by truck.

It would be the first time Blue would ever fly— without his own wings supporting him in the air. Mark wondered what he would think of his ride.

Blue was agitated. He did not want to be put in the carrier. Mark and Timmie were concerned as the sleek bird pressed himself against the mesh and tried to find a way out of the box.

"That's a good sign," said Mr. Faraday, "I hope he keeps that spirit all the way to the starting field."

Mark wasn't so sure. He was afraid that Blue would have himself worn out before the race ever started.

When all of the paper work was done, Blue was taken from the boys and carried through the door to the room where he would be kept until boarding time. Mark and Timmie could hear other homers as the door opened and closed. They stared at the closed door that had shut them off from Blue, and turned to follow their mother, Dr. Mike, and Mr. Faraday, back toward the cars.

Mr. Faraday had six birds entered in the race. There had been seven, but one was scratched at the last minute because it didn't appear to be in top form.

"When will he get back?" asked Timmie of Mr. Faraday as they walked side by side.

"It's hard to tell. On a long flight like this, so many things affect their time. The weather. The food supply. They need to rest. They need water. There can be hawks and—."

But he got no further.

"Hawks?"

"Blue has handled hawks before. Remember the time we took him out west for that short test flight? Remember the hawk that showed up and how Blue took cover right away? Blue is smart about hawks. He'll watch for 'em."

Timmie felt some better, but the word 'hawk' still filled his heart with fear. Yet he had watched Blue. Blue had been smart alright. He went under cover and never moved a muscle until the hawk was gone—and then he headed home to the cote in a straight line as fast as he could fly. Timmie smiled, just remembering it.

He slipped a hand into the knarled hand of the old man. Mr. Faraday squeezed the hand—just a bit.

"Mr. Faraday," said Timmie in not much more than a whisper, "do you think that Blue could win first?"

Mr. Faraday's eyes widened.

"So—gettin' greedy now are we? I thought that we had talked about—."

"I know—but—if he really wanted to, do you think that he is strong enough and—and smart enough—and *drive—drive* enough, to come first?"

Mr. Faraday shook his head. He hesitated.

"So you want an honest answer, eh? The opinion of an old fancier?"

"Yeah," prompted Timmie.

Mr. Faraday stopped his walking and turned to look at the small boy.

"Don't you tell anyone I said this," he whispered, "but that bird of yours—if he has him a fair race and no interferences—he is capable of doing anything he wants to. First? He could leave all the others in his air trail."

Timmie was about to whoop when Mr. Faraday placed a hand of caution lightly over his mouth. But the old man didn't stop the childish eyes from shining.

Blue might do even better than sixth—or even fourth. Blue might even come in first.

Chapter Seventeen

Blue

Blue had never objected to the carrier before. But then he had never been a father before—a father with responsibilities. He needed to be home—home at the cote helping Josie to care for their young. But try as he might, there seemed to be no way to get himself free of the carrier box.

Other pigeons were all around him. They, too, were in their carrier boxes. Most of them seemed excited. Many of them had already learned that the carrier box meant another race—and races were exciting, even though one never knew the hours of flight that must be endured. Still, it was a challenge, and the birds welcomed it.

Blue would have welcomed it also, had he not sensed that it was all wrong for him to be there. What would Josie think? Would she feel deserted? Would she be able to handle the two hungry squabs all alone? Blue fretted and stewed, but his situation did not change. He became agitated—and it increased with each passing minute.

If Mr. Faraday could have observed the bird, he might have doubted his method of increasing Blue's desire to hurry home. Like Mark had said, Blue might be all worn out before the flight ever started.

Even Blue realized that he must conserve some strength. There would be a long trip in the carrier. Then there would be the release—and he would be free to fly back home—back to Josic and his young—but who knew just how long that flight might be? Hours maybe. Most of the day. More than a day? Even the thought of it made Blue more upset.

Blue had no way of knowing that the flight, at best, would take him four or five days. And at worst, Blue would never reach home and Josie at all.

He tried to quiet his racing heart and relax against the softness of the carrier floor. Next door two young cocks were talking.

"I had pretty good time in the last race," the check was saying. "I heard my man boasting about it."

The other cock tilted his head, and his beady eyes looked amused, yet defiant.

"Last races don't count," he challenged, "it's always 'this' race. 'This' is the race that you concentrate on. What you gonna do with 'this' race?"

The check took the challenge.

"What am I gonna do? My strategy is my own, and I give away no secrets. But I tell you one thing I'm gonna do. I'm gonna beat you." And so saying, he turned his back on the other cock and began picking at the mesh of his carrier.

The second cock, a mealy, grinned a lopsided grin, and looked over at Blue.

"Got a loudmouth here," he said. "He's gonna lick all of us."

"I heard," said Blue. He looked back at the check.

He looked like he could fly alright. Blue shrugged. Maybe he would beat them—but he wouldn't be going home to Josie. Blue began to work at the mesh on his cage also.

The ride seemed unreasonably long. Blue pressed himself against the mesh, listening to the sounds around them. The roar of the engine sounded different from the trucks he was used to. The 'feel' was different, too. Not the bumps and jostles, but dips and weaves. This ride was different, Blue could feel that. But it was still long—and it was irritating. When would they ever see sky again? When would they be released from their carriers? Blue wondered just how long it had been since he had left Josie and his cote.

At last there was a soft bump, and their forward motion stopped. All around him Blue heard the excited conversation of the pigeons as they discussed the fact that they must be near their destination. The check and the mealy were still eying one another and exchanging barbs and challenges. Blue couldn't be bothered with such cheap rivalry.

On the other side of him two older cocks, obviously from the same loft, discussed the coming race.

"Must be a fair distance," said the first one. "Anytime we take this flyer we have a good ways to get back home."

"How you planning to handle the flight?" asked the second one. "You staying with the populated areas or are you going for the open country?"

"I'll have to take a look around first. Depends on the situation. If the populated area means lots of smog, I'll probably go around it."

"Me, too. I hate that smog."

"Just hope we don't hit a thunderstorm."

"I've found that it's best just to sit those out if they

don't last too long. The beating that you take trying to fly through a storm slows you down more in the long run than just waiting it out and then flying on. They take a lot of your strength and energy, those storms."

Blue had never flown through a thunderstorm before. He tucked away that bit of information for future reference.

At long last they were unloaded—checked and reloaded. This time to a van, and then they were off to—somewhere. Somewhere. Blue had no way of knowing where—but home—his cote—and Josie—were 'that' way. Blue could sense it. He knew exactly the direction he must take to return to them.

At last the van stopped, and the doors were opened. Carrier after carrier filled with homers was lifted from the van. There were handlers who took out each bird, examined it carefully, and announced whether it would be taking part in the race or not. Only a few of the birds were disqualified.

Blue happened to see three of the members from Mr. Faraday's loft. They greeted one another excitedly. It was good to see someone from the home area.

"We'll keep an eye out for you on the return trip," called the spotted cock, and Blue nodded his head in appreciation.

Then the younger cock called out good-naturedly, "When I get home I'll let them know that you are on the way."

Blue laughed, but he didn't really think that it was funny. He planned to be the first one home.

The birds could sense that the start of the race was getting near. Their leg bands were checked to make sure they were on securely, and then handlers examined their bodies and wings one last time. Finally—finally—they were released into the air, and a great cheer went

up from the crowd on the ground. The race was on.

Blue had never seen so many pairs of wings. All around him was their whirr and flutter. His first thought was to separate himself from the mass so he might be able to look around and get his bearings. He needed to sort out his course of flight, not his direction—he knew that instinctively.

Slowly, the whirling mass began to untangle, and Blue began to fly away from the other birds.

Carefully he studied the scene beneath him. There were mostly open fields. Off to his right, huge buildings lifted themselves skyward. Various streams of colored smoke boiled forth from the smokestacks. Blue would avoid that. He would fly around, rather than over the city, even if it did lie directly in his path.

There was a natural course that seemed to follow the river as it wound west. Blue decided to take it for a while. He swung around quickly and started home. All of the other birds were still circling, choosing their routes.

The first several miles of flying went well. Blue lost his first burst of agitated energy and settled into a steady pace that kept him well ahead of the rest of the homers. He did not look behind him. It was no concern whether he was ahead or not; he only desired to get to Josie as soon as he was able.

Evening came. Blue knew he must take cover. He had already been flying for hours. He needed water. He needed nourishment. He needed rest. But he hated to take the time for any of them.

At last he grounded. He had spied a small stream and knew it would supply him with at least one of his needs. He drank deeply, feeling the cool water restoring his small body.

He had not needed to forage much on his other flights. Most of them had been rather short 'hops', and he knew there would be his special grain mix waiting for him at the cote. But he sensed this this flight might be different, and that he should not let his energy be depleted because of lack of food. The old birds had spoken of a long flight—and they should know, having competed in many races during their lifetimes.

So Blue foraged until he was quite satisfied. By then the darkness had closed in around him. He found a perch well off the ground and among the thick branches of a tree, tucked his head under his wing, and slept.

Blue didn't know it, but as he fed and rested, the check passed him a mile to his right. The young bird was determined to be victorious in the race and had waived the necessity of feeding properly and resting as early as he should have. He was strong. He had endurance. He would 'tough it out', he decided, and be first bird in.

Chapter Eighteen

Difficulties

The next day went well for Blue. He had fed and rested at night and took a refreshing drink of water in the morning before beginning his day. His strength was sustained, his wings felt great. He would have enjoyed the flight had his thoughts not been so totally on Josie and the nest of young ones. He longed for the comfort and protection of the cote, as well—and he even missed the humans.

On the third morning he flew into bad weather. A thundercloud moved toward him, and he knew it was useless to try to fly around it. It spread across much of the western sky. He remembered the words of the older birds and flew into the storm only until it picked up fury. Soon he sheltered, crowding closely to the trunk of a huge pine tree where the wind and rain could not beat upon him.

The storm lasted for about four long hours. Blue chaffed at the lost time, but he held himself in check. It would be foolish to try to buck the strong wind and heavy rain.

At last Blue was able to take to the air again; he traveled faster, knowing he did not need to conserve his strength. Darkness would soon come, and he could rest then.

He had not flown for long when he noticed another homer ahead of him. He knew that it must be one of the birds from the race and his excitement mounted. Could it possibly be one of Mr. Faraday's birds? Perhaps they could shelter together and catch up on some news of the racers. Blue strengthened his forward thrust.

It was the check who was ahead of him—Blue recognized him as he closed the gap between them, and then—just as he was ready to call out a greeting to the other bird—he saw something else. A movement—just a flash—to his right. Blue jerked his head around just in time to see a hawk lift himself off the top of a jagged, dead spruce tree and swoop toward them.

Blue cried an alarm to the check and veered sharply to the left seeking cover, but the check had expended himself. He had unwisely pushed himself through the storm and was already weary from not resting as long as he should have at night. His energy and agility were depleted. He tried to veer away from the hawk, but there was no strength left for the additional push. Blue watched, sickeningly, as the check was picked from the sky.

It was a long time before Blue could coax himself back into the sky. The vision of the hawk kept flashing before him. He could hear again the cries of the check pigeon as the hawk lifted him up—up—beyond the skies where the pigeons flew.

Finally, Blue's trembling stopped. He steeled himself against his terror. The thought of Josie and the home cote drove him onward again. Now, he was far more cautious as he flew. He knew the hours spent in rest were not wasted hours. He also knew firsthand, the wisdom of resting out the storm. He pressed onward, determining to fly not just by might—but by wisdom.

Mark and Timmie knew it was foolish, but from the third day on they began to watch the skies. No bird could possibly make the flight in that length of time, but they studied the eastern horizon anyway.

Josie fussed and fretted in her pen, but then she settled down to care for her two babies. The squabs took so much of her time and attention that she scarcely had time to think of anything else. The boys tried to help her, but there was no way they could take over the feeding chores. Somehow Josie managed, but the boys secretly wondered who would be the happiest to see the return of Blue—his anxious owners, or his harried mate?

Another storm moved in during the night and was still there when Blue awoke the next morning. He remembered the day before and the incident with the hawk. He knew it was foolish to spend all his energy fighting against bad weather, so he fed some, had a drink from a small puddle, and groomed his feathers.

The storm still persisted, and after what seemed like hours of feeling frustrated and upset, Blue decided to take to the sky. Perhaps a few miles of flying would take him beyond the storm.

It was not that easy. The rain clouds seemed to be covering miles and miles of the land below. The wind was not strong like it had been in the thunderstorm, and Blue decided to put in a few hours of flying through the rain. He would not tire himself, he promised, and he would not forget to keep a sharp lookout for hawks.

He flew on. The rain beat steadily against his breast, and rolled off the feathers of his back. He knew instinctively that he was not making good time, but at least he was making some forward progress. He was not sitting idly, agitated at being grounded.

Blue was weary when he stopped for the day—weary, and a bit careless. He dropped to the ground without thought of a water supply. With the rain falling steadily, there would be water enough most anywhere, he reasoned.

He was busying himself hunting for food when he was startled by a flash of movement behind him. Without even waiting for a glimpse of what the creature might be, Blue spread his wings and thrust himself forward. He was almost fast enough as the mouth of whatever animal had been out to get him closed with a snap on Blue's tail feathers. A fraction of a second delay would have cost Blue his life.

The damaged tail feathers were serious enough. The tail acted as Blue's rudder and kept him on even keel in the sky. There was little pain connected with the mishap—but Blue found that he was hampered in flying the next day.

To make matters worse, the mild wind that was blowing came out of the northwest. Blue wanted to fly directly west and that meant he had to fight the wind every mile of the way. Even though the rains had finally stopped, the wind that beat constantly against him made flying very difficult. His tail just did not work properly with its missing and damaged feathers, and what Blue could normally have coped with very nicely now became a problem.

Still, he sensed he was getting closer and closer to Josie, but would he be able to fight off the wind enough to get back on track?

As he traveled on, his tail affecting his flight, Blue found he was tiring more easily. He had to put extra effort into holding himself on course.

He had avoided another city, and his flight took him over acres and acres of emptiness—or at least it looked empty to Blue. He did see some creatures feeding in large herds, and he did pass over farm buildings and fields, but Blue didn't pay too much attention to the scenes beneath him. Instead, he kept his eyes on the skies.

He watched for hawks in particular. He also watched for other homers. He wondered just where all the birds were that had started their flight at the same time. Little did Blue know that despite his difficulties, he still was leading the birds home.

It was late afternoon when Blue's world blew apart. He was just beginning to give consideration to sheltering for the night, when he noticed activity beneath him. It was men who tramped the bushes below him—men, and a couple of the small creatures that often ran with men. Blue paid little attention to them and kept on flying. He would do another mile or so and then stop for the night, he decided.

And then there was a loud 'boom'. Blue felt himself lift and then fall. Next, he was hurtling headlong toward the earth, a sharp pain seering through his left wing.

Somehow Blue managed to fight against gravity and get himself upright. He could not gain full control of the wing, but he did manage to use it in some measure to stop his downward plunge. Then he veered to his left and sustained flight long enough to ease himself to earth and light with some measure of control.

He could hear the commotion of the men and their creatures. They were coming toward him, tramping through the bushes and the grass, their cries filling the air with frightening noises. Blue forced himself to his feet and pushed himself forward. He must fly. He must! But he couldn't fly. He must hide! But where? Yet he knew that his very life depended upon keeping out of the reach of the men and their creatures.

The damaged wing was a liability. Besides causing

him pain, it would not function properly, and Blue could not fold it up out of the way so that he could run. He could hear the creatures closely behind him, and he pushed himself forward with determined effort, his heart pounding within his breast. They were so close, and he still had found no place to hide. And then, just ahead, Blue spotted a fallen tree with a hollow in its trunk. He increased his speed and thrust himself into the trunk as far as he could push his body into its depths.

It proved to be good enough. He dropped to a resting position inside the rotting tree trunk, totally exhausted from his run, his pounding heart hammering within his small body as the noise of the men and barking of the creatures filled the air all around him.

At last they gave up. Blue could hear their steps getting farther and farther away. He knew they were finally leaving. He also knew he was in a terrible situation. The wing still throbbed with pain and wouldn't respond right when he tried to move it. He was thirsty and tired, and he had not eaten.

And yet the only thought that really occupied his mind was that he needed to get home. He crouched in the darkness of the log and tried to relax his body in spite of his pain. For now, he could do nothing but rest. Perhaps, with time, the wing would heal. Blue closed his eyes and tried to sleep. For the time being, he was thankful for the fallen tree. He felt a measure of safety there. He would rest awhile, wait for healing, and then go home to Josie.

When Blue awoke after a restless night, he was still in pain. His wing now felt stiff and useless. He tried to move it but a sharp pain stopped him. He tried to settle himself more comfortably so that he could sleep again. It did not work. His stomach reminded him that he had not eaten for some time. He knew he had to forage.

He would never mend if he didn't have nourishment. But he feared leaving the log since he was totally defenseless. A bird who could not fly could not expect to stay out of the claws of predators.

Slowly, Blue backed himself up so he could escape the confines of the log, though he feared exposing himself to the world in such a way. To his surprise he discovered one place within the log where the hollow was wide enough for him to turn himself around. He felt better about entering the world head first. At least he would have the advantage of peering out to see if any predators were in sight.

He moved slowly forward, guarding carefully his injured wing, when he noticed something else. A small animal must have housed itself in the log before him, for off to one side of the opening was a little pile of grain and seeds that had been stored there.

Blue could hardly believe the find. He ate hungrily of the store until he felt quite satisfied. "Now, if only I had a drink," he thought, "I might be able to sleep."

A morning shower provided the drink. It also showed Blue that the log was not waterproof. Soon its floor was damp and uncomfortable. Blue hated the wetness, but there was no other place to go. He pushed himself as high out of the water as he could and settled to do some sleeping.

Overhead—one by one—the other homers continued their journey, passing over Blue and his damaged wing as they traveled home.

Not all the homers finished the trip. The check was lost to the hawk, and eleven other birds did not finish the flight. One of them was found at another loft some days later, and one band was turned in by a farmer who found it on his property. The others were never heard of again.

At home, the boys continued to watch the sky. The days went by slowly. Surely it was time for Blue to be getting home. They could not play, could not sleep, and could scarcely eat, as they waited for their bird.

Mr. Faraday had been closely following the weather reports as he waited for the return of the birds. He knew the eastern storms would delay the birds and was quick to inform the two boys. He wanted to relieve them of any anxiety he possibly could.

"The storms will slow them down some," he told Mark and Timmie. "But they'll be smart enough to sit 'em out. Be here a day or so later, that's all."

It was hard for the boys to accept the additional time, and they still could not keep from watching the eastern horizon.

Then one day a bird was seen in the sky. But it was Silver Wings, a member of Mr. Faraday's loft that landed. Then a number of hours later, Blue Boy the First and Mr. Sam came in almost together.

Over the next day the other members of Mr. Faraday's loft also returned, but still no Blue. The boys began to worry now. Even Mr. Faraday looked concerned, though he made no such comment to the boys. Blue would not be a winner, that was obvious. He certainly wouldn't take first. He wouldn't even be fourth or sixth. In fact, he would not even be in the top twenty.

The boys forgot about the prize money. Now they just longed for Blue to make it home. Blue, who had been in their nightly prayers ever since he had become their bird, now became an urgent request.

But the days slipped by slowly, one by one. Timmie stopped putting the marks on the calendar. Even Mr. Faraday admitted defeat and suggested that the boys pick another young cock from among the birds. The boys balked. It wouldn't seem loyal to Blue, somehow.

They decided to wait awhile.

Mrs. Thomas knew how the boys were hurting. She longed to help them, but there really wasn't much she could do or say. One night she heard the whispering from their bedroom and went in to have a chat with her heartbroken sons.

She perched on the side of Timmie's bed and took his hand. They all remained silent for a few minutes as Mrs. Thomas sought for words that might bring comfort.

"Mr. Faraday has sent out notices to all of the lofts along the route. All of the fanciers are watching for Blue," said Mrs. Thomas quietly. "Maybe we'll still find him."

Mark stirred in the bunk above them.

It was encouraging to think there might still be hope.

"We won't win any money though," interjected Timmie.

"The money really wasn't that important," went on Mrs. Thomas. "We are getting along just fine without it."

Mark sighed. They were getting along okay, he guessed, but they sure could have used the money. Why, he had heard his mom and Dr. Mike talking just the other day about the old car she drove to work and the family used for church and grocery shopping. It was just about ready to give up—and Mark knew there wasn't even money for repairs, let alone a new car.

He sighed again.

It was Timmie who spoke.

"We thought if we made enough money, you might be able to stay home with us instead of working," he said sadly.

"Do you really want me home that much?" asked Mrs. Thomas in a choked voice.

Timmie hesitated. Would it make his mom feel

unhappy if he admitted his need for her?

"It would be nice," he said softly.

"Well," said Mrs. Thomas slowly. "There might still be a way."

Mark sat up in bed so he could listen more carefully, and Timmie searched his mother's face in the soft glow of the dresser lamp.

"You see," said Mrs. Thomas, a light beginning to shine in her eyes, "Dr. Mike has asked me to marry him. Should we?"

Mark could not contain himself. He bounded down from the top bunk and threw his arms around his mother. Timmie jerked up into a sitting position and hugged her, too. Then Mark had an awful thought.

"Would we have to move?" he asked soberly.

Mark's words brought Timmie back to reality. A move would mean no cote. A move would mean no pigeons. A move would mean no Blue—ever. He held his breath.

"As a matter of fact," said Mrs. Thomas with laughter in her voice, "Mike has asked Mr. Faraday if he can buy this part of the acreage. He wants to stay right here—and build an addition onto this house."

"What did Mr. Faraday say?" asked the boys in unison.

Mrs. Thomas smiled and pulled her sons close.

"He said he'd like us for neighbors," she said happily.

Both boys cheered wildly.

"Then let's get married," shouted Timmie. "Let's get married. Then we won't just have a friend—we'll have a dad!"

Chapter Nineteen

The Finish

Blue did not know how many days he had hidden in the log. He knew the stored grain and seed supply was all gone and that he was hungry. He knew he would need to leave the log in order to find nourishment, but his wing was still not healed sufficiently for flight.

He put it off as long as he dared and then forced himself to advance carefully and slowly from his shelter.

It was almost dark when he first made his appearance. Darkness meant night prowlers to Blue, and he was unable to lift himself to a perch above the ground.

He searched frantically for seeds to fill his stomach, and before he was even satisfied, he hurried back to the safety of the log.

After a fairly restful sleep, Blue again emerged and foraged for food. He even found water and satisfied his thirst. The pockets of rainwater that had gathered in the log earlier had dried up, and so Blue's inside water supply was now expended.

He had to travel farther for water than he would have liked. Blue knew the closer he could remain to the log the safer he would be.

Each time after eating and drinking, Blue would hurry back to the log as fast as his short legs could carry him.

His strong urge to get home was still prodding him, but Blue knew he could not fly. It was hard to keep returning to the log each day. The log, though safe, never got him any nearer to Josie. Blue chaffed under the necessity of remaining stationary.

He began to exercise his stiff and sore wing. At first there was little movement at all, but gradually, ever so gradually, Blue began to get a little action back in the limb.

Each day he worked harder and more persistently. Finally, he even dared to propel himself into the air. It didn't work well. After a few frantic beats in the air, he was right back where he had started from—on the ground. But Blue did not give up, and in a few days' time he found he could actually lift himself into the air.

It was a good start. Now Blue could rest on a perch, and he didn't feel so vulnerable. He dared to venture away from his log. He would soon start home again.

The first miles were painful and slow. Blue could only fly a very short distance, and then he would be forced to rest. But always he pressed on—and on. He was heading home! He was returning to his cote! He was going back to Josie and his young!

With his heart pounding fiercely, he would lift himself into the air. He fought with all his might to stay airborne and drummed the air frantically to stay on course.

His damaged wing made flying a straight course much more difficult. He would forget to compensate with his good wing and found himself continually veering to the left.

The urge to return home was so strong within Blue

that he could not even relax between short flights. Hammering away in his brain was the desire to get back to Josie and his cote. He even walked for short distances when he was too tired to fly. He did not forsake caution. He knew that on the ground he was in danger, so his sharp eyes studied carefully every inch of the terrain around him as he pressed on. He was going home! He was going home!

Day by day, Blue's wing strengthened until he could fly for a few hours at a time. And then, the glad day came when he recognized some landmarks. He had flown this sky before. He was nearing his destination. The excitement poured new energy into his body. One last burst of determination pushed him on. It wouldn't be long now. He would make it!

He flew on, his body straining and pushing forward with every beat of his wings. He had little reserve left but he knew that the cote was just beyond the distant clump of trees. He knew—he knew where he was. He knew that shelter and food and Josie awaited him just ahead. He forced his wings to keep on beating even though his eyes were glazed from fatigue, and his body ached with every movement.

Many days had passed. Mark and Timmie had *almost* given up. Mr. Faraday, their mother and the kind doctor, who was soon to be their new father, *had* all given up. The boys didn't know if Josie had given up or not. Her two squabs were feathered now and almost ready to leave the nest. There should have been two new babies in the nest with Josie, but she didn't seem to worry about that.

Their mother's approaching wedding had helped some in getting the boys' thoughts off Blue and onto other things. Still, they secretly longed for their homer. Their very first homer—and they were both quite convinced that there would never be another pigeon quite like their Blue.

Mr. Faraday had again suggested that the boys pick a new cock from his loft.

"Why?" asked Timmie innocently. "Don't you think that Blue will want to race again?

Mr. Faraday hardly knew how to answer the young boy. He didn't want to smash all his hopes.

"Well, sure—sure—," he sputtered. "If—when—Blue makes it home, he'll probably race again."

"Then what do you mean?" asked Mark. "Do you think he isn't a good racer because he didn't win?"

"Oh, no! Oh, no!" Mr. Faraday was quick to assure them. "I think Blue was—is—is a great racer. And havin' problems in a race—things that make it tough to get home—why that only makes a homer even smarter—and stronger for the next race."

"Then we'll just wait for Blue," said Mark. Timmie nodded his head in agreement and Mr. Faraday reluctantly let the matter drop.

And then one day the most amazing thing happened as Timmie and Mark were caring for Josie. Timmie's eyes lifted to the sky—as their eyes did every day ever so many times, and he squinted against the sun, shading his eyes with his hand.

"What's the matter?" asked Mark.

"I thought I saw a bird."

"Prob'ly a jay or a robin," said Mark, not wanting to get his hopes up.

"Looked like a pigeon—just beyond those trees. Can't see it now."

"One of Mr. Faraday's," responded Mark as he went back to cleaning Josie's pen.

"They don't fly alone like that," said Timmie, pretending to forget the bird.

He didn't. Whenever he could steal another unnoticed look eastward, he did. The bird emerged from behind the screen of woods and flew on toward them. It was coming their way alright. Directly. And it wasn't a jay or a robin. It *was* a pigeon.

Timmie waited for the bird to get closer.

Was it—? Could it be—? Surely not, but it sure looked like him. Though Blue always flew much smoother than that, but still—? Timmie's heart began to hammer within his chest. He could hardly keep from crying out to Mark. But what if he was wrong? What if it wasn't Blue?

At last Timmie could stand it no longer. But he didn't yell. His voice was no more than a whisper.

"Mark," he said, his voice choking up. "Mark, I think it's him!"

Mark spun around and looked in the direction that Timmie's finger was pointing. Instinctively, he reached out and pulled his younger brother to him. They both stood breathless, watching as the weary and travel-worn Blue propelled himself determinedly the last several feet through the summer air and made a rather ungraceful descent to the cote.

"Look!" whispered Mark, the tears streaming down his cheeks. "Look! He's home. It's Blue!"

Blue tilted his head to survey his cote and hesitated only a moment. Then rather awkwardly, because of his extreme weariness, he went in to see Josie and his young.

With a wild shout the two brothers raced for the house, all silence and caution thrown to the wind.

"Mom! Mr. Faraday!" they screamed. "He's home! Blue's home! Honest! He's home! It's our Blue. He made it! He made it! Blue's home!"